Monte picked up one of the strawberries and held it out in front of him

Torie looked up at him and opened her mouth to receive the fruit. Monte rubbed it along the outline of her lips before placing it in her awaiting mouth. Torie closed her lips around the berry, but did not bite down. Instead, she sucked it firmly and then released it. Monte's mouth fell open as he stared at her.

Torie stuck out her tongue and licked the fruit in a circular motion. She let her tongue dance around its tip and then its entire circumference, before closing her mouth over it again. This time she bit down and removed a large chunk of the ripe berry. She moved closer to Monte with juice dripping down from her bottom lip. He leaned in, catching her mouth in his. They kissed until the strawberry was gone. They disengaged from their fiery kiss and Torie placed both hands on Monte's shoulders and pushed him backward until he was lying on his back. She swung her left leg over his body and straddled him. She sat down on his upper thighs and, though he tried to pull her up higher to make contact with his throbbing manhood, she wouldn't budge.

"Patience," she said.

Books by Kim Shaw

Kimani Romance

*Forever, for Always,
   for Love*
Soul Caress
Romance Backstage
Lift Me Higher

Kimani Arabesque

Pack Light
Free Verse
Love's Portrait

KIM SHAW

is a high school English teacher in New Jersey, where she resides with her husband and two children. In addition to writing and teaching, she is working on a literacy project aimed at improving reading and cultural awareness in her community.

Lift ME HIGHER

KIM SHAW

Lift Me Higher is dedicated to people who are more interested in what they can do to uplift others than in how they themselves can benefit. You know who you are.

3 1967 01195 4545

KIMANI PRESS™

Recycling programs for this product may not exist in your area.

ISBN-13: 978-0-373-86159-0

LIFT ME HIGHER

www.kimanipress.com

Printed in U.S.A.

Dear Reader,

I wrote *Lift Me Higher* because I wanted to look at a relationship from the male perspective. Too often attention is paid to the single mother and how difficult it is for her to balance family, career and passion. *Lift Me Higher* asks, "what about the single father?" Men are burdened with the expectation that they be strong and unsusceptible to heartache. Monte Lewis shows that a real man is one who can put it down on the job and at home, while still being human and vulnerable. He's a man who knows that with a real woman by his side, there is nothing he can't do. I hope you enjoy his story.

Currently, I am working on several different things. There are so many interesting characters taking up space in my brain—like the sexy firefighter who likes his women as hot as his fires, until he gets burned, or the grocery clerk turned lottery winner who finds that true love doesn't need a bunch of zeroes on the end! I continue to write to entertain, enlighten and inform, and I thank you for your continued readership.

Sincerely,

Kim Shaw

Chapter 1

Simply Stunning

Monte scanned the day's calendar on his PDA as he moved toward the elevator bank for floors twenty through thirty-one of midtown Manhattan's Time Warner building. He adjusted his red tie and smoothed the lapels of his midnight-blue Brooks Brothers suit absently, thinking about all he had to do in the day ahead of him. The lobby area was just beginning to buzz with activity at seven forty-five on a Tuesday morning. Monte had an eight-thirty meeting and a string of conference calls to follow. It would be a busy day as usual, through which he would plow tirelessly, making deals come together seamlessly. No matter, he thought, because by five o'clock Monte would call it quits for the day. His boys had a Little League game that evening and, with him being their coach as well, it definitely wouldn't do for him to be late.

Monte opened the *Daily News* paper he'd tucked beneath his arm, turning to the sports section. The ding of the elevator as it landed on the lobby floor and its doors opening drew Monte's attention. He stepped into the elevator, pressed the button marked twenty-seven and became engrossed in the paper again. Absorbed in the highlights of the Nets' latest

Cinderella victory, Monte didn't look up as another passenger entered the elevator just before the doors closed. The car began its smooth ascent and Monte's senses were suddenly assailed by the faint yet sweet scent of lilies. His eyes followed his nose and they led him to slender feet clad in six-inch stilettos, up stockingless, shapely brown calves to a stunning black skirt that stopped midthigh and hugged sinfully curvaceous hips.

Monte swallowed as his eyes continued their journey, taking their sweet time. The torso of this magnificent vision was held securely by a black suit jacket and its top button stopped at a bustline that begged for attention. Above a pearl-necklace-adorned graceful neck was the face of an angel. Hazel eyes met Monte's, and he was at once embarrassed at his voyeurism and enthralled by her beauty.

Monte opened his mouth to speak, but before he could command control over his vocabulary, the elevator came to a halt and, with a chime, the doors opened. The alluring woman exited, without as much as another glance at Monte, who remained dumbfounded and immobile.

Monte had always prided himself on being a man who was not easily moved by a pretty face and, had she been just that, Monte probably would not have given her more than an appreciative nod. Yet, there was more to the woman than just physical beauty. There was an ethereal essence that seeped from the inside out, and a presence that had captivated him. He could only liken the experience to being caught in a spider's web, hopelessly entangled in the strong fiber. It was not until the doors closed again and the elevator continued its ascent that he came to his senses and realized that the floor the woman had exited on was also his floor, the twenty-seventh. He quickly depressed a button for one of the higher floors, exited and caught another car headed down.

"Who was that woman who just got off of the elevator?" Monte asked the receptionist when he'd landed at the office space of Cooper & Beardsley. The entertainment-law firm had been home to Monte for the past six years and he'd been a senior associate for the past two.

Monte's immediate investigation uncovered that the beautiful woman he'd been ogling in the elevator was one of his firm's newest clients, Torie Turner, a model turned actress whose career was, by all accounts, poised to take off. After spending years as a print model, she'd decided to take her career to the next level, building an impressive résumé along the way. Over the past few years she'd done a number of small theater productions, a few commercials and had recently completed the pilot episode for a new television series. Like many new-millennium actors, Torie had opted to replace the services of an agent at fifteen to twenty percent with an entertainment-law firm offering headhunting, contract negotiations and other legal services at a lower cost per diem. Torie Turner was as smart as she was beautiful, and after careful consideration, she'd hired the Cooper & Beardsley firm, with junior associate Monica Schwartz as the lead attorney, to review the contracts and offers that were beginning to come her way.

Monte knew instantly that he'd never had the pleasure of seeing any of Torie's work because, if he had, he doubted seriously he would have ever been able to get her out of his head. Distracted, and uncharacteristically nervous, Monte kept one eye on his work all morning and the other on the closed door of the conference room where Torie's meeting was taking place. His plan was to spring into action the moment the door opened and casually saunter in her direction. He hadn't figured out what he would say to her, but hoped the words would come to him when needed.

The persistent flutters in Monte's gut kept him on edge. He felt abnormal and quite unlike himself, as if he were having an out-of-body experience. While Monte had never considered himself a ladies' man in any sense of the term, in his youth he'd never had a problem in that department. At thirty-five years old, Monte had successfully become what is commonly referred to as an *IBM*. This ideal black man had worked hard to establish security in his career, become financially fit and was also well traveled. Intellectually stimulating, good-natured and articulate were adjectives to which he was well suited. Finally, Monte's six feet three inches of velvet black skin and well-maintained physique made him the complete package. Monte had yet to meet the person, male or female, with whom he could not hold his own on any level, which was why he was completely thrown for a loop that this Torie Turner might actually be that person who made him feel less than self-assured, and he steadied himself to dispel that possibility at the first chance he got.

However, when the door finally opened and Monte spotted Torie from his vantage point across the corridor, he continued to sit immobile. His mind raced as he tried to force himself into motion, but his nerves held him captive. Deflated, Monte realized that it had been years—seven to be exact—since he had approached a woman to whom he felt an attraction. His late wife, Shawna, was the last woman he'd ever made an advance on or struck up a casual conversation with regarding anything on a personal level, and Monte realized that he was sorely out of practice. To make matters worse, he felt like an idiot as he sat watching her disappear down the corridor with pretty-boy Matthew Sampson trotting alongside of her and beaming that twenty-thousand-dollar cash-and-carry smile of his. Monte resolved that perhaps it wasn't meant to be, acknowledging that he would have felt even more idiotic if he had approached her in front of Matthew and the entire office of his colleagues and found himself tongue-tied. Worse, he might have said something foolish, prompting her to laugh in his face.

Monte cast off his designs on the opulent woman, chiding himself for even considering approaching her. He had a full life, he reminded himself. With the care of his two young sons and his ailing mother as his number-one priorities, along with building a secure and successful career, Monte felt he didn't have time for any distractions. Besides, he reasoned, what right had he to ask for more?

Irritated and disappointed, Monte plowed through the rest of his day, determined to forget about Torie Turner. It proved to be a feat next to impossible.

Chapter 2

You Can't Have It All

"Mama, I already told you that I'm done with the commercials and, for now at least, the stage. I'm concentrating on television and movie scripts, period. Why can't you get that?"

Torie stabbed at a piece of lettuce in the Cobb salad in front of her and glared at her mother. It was just after two o'clock in the afternoon and the two women were seated inside of Braserie, a French restaurant in midtown, having a late lunch.

"Torie, I just don't want to see you put all of your eggs in one basket," Brenda replied.

"Mama, if I want to be successful at this, I have to focus on one thing. I can't commit to a theater production and still go out on casting calls."

"But, Torie, you read all the time about how limited the roles are for black actresses in movies. I mean, honey, you have to face the fact that there are a lot of talented, pretty girls out there trying to land that next big movie."

Torie took a deep breath. Dealing with her mother had always been a trial. No matter what Torie felt or wanted, it seemed to her as if her mother's sole purpose in life was to feel or want something different for her. For all of her childhood and much of her young adult life, Torie had acquiesced to her mother's wishes, but no more. Torie had moved to New York from Atlanta with two purposes in mind—one, to establish her career, and two, to put some distance between her life and her mother's controlling habits.

"Mama, can't we just enjoy lunch…enjoy your visit and not get into this again? Just trust me for a change. I know what I'm doing, and besides, if it doesn't work out, I can always get another commercial or play," Torie said, looking at her mother imploringly.

Brenda Turner considered her daughter. There were times, like this one, where Brenda winced at the sight of her daughter. Torie was beautiful and, in her face, Brenda saw herself. In her youth, Brenda had been equally as stunning and, she felt, twice as ambitious. She'd wanted so much for herself and had planned on touring the world as a famous jazz singer. Brenda had thought that she could have it all—the career, the fame and the family. She'd married Torie's father at twenty-one years old, despite her own mother's misgivings. She'd been singing at local nightclubs in the southeast and had been putting together an arrangement to work with Miles Davis and Herbie Hancock on an upcoming collaboration. Her husband, Hanif Turner, was also involved in the music business as a saxophone player, although considered by most to be just a mediocre talent. Yet, they were happy and excited about their futures, and Hanif was very supportive of Brenda's musical ambitions. That's why when Brenda discovered that she was pregnant, neither of them was overjoyed. Due to irregular periods and virtually no symptoms, Brenda was almost six months along by the time she realized that she was expecting. Brenda's dreams, along with her marriage, paid the price under the strain of caring for their child.

"I just want you to maximize on your opportunities while you still can," Brenda said now, casting her eyes down to the grilled salmon and steamed asparagus in front of her.

The underlying message of Brenda's statement was not lost on Torie. She'd always noticed the faraway look that came into her mother's eyes when she was washing the dinner dishes, vacuuming or undertaking some other mundane task. Torie was still a relatively young child when she'd come to understand what that look on her mother's face meant. Motherhood had been an unexpected hitch in her mother's life plan. There was no way Brenda could have known that her first child, a boy named Miles by his young parents, would have been born with a congenital birth defect that they would spend the first five years of his life fighting. Torie was one year old when Miles succumbed to his disease and, by then, Brenda's dreams of a career in music had shriveled up and died.

"Mama, please don't worry. Trust me. I know what I'm doing. You'll see," Torie said, looking at her mother in a meaningful way.

"All right, well, tell me about these lawyers you hired. How was your meeting? Did you have a good feeling about them?" Brenda asked.

"Oh, the firm is one of the best—a lot of heavy hitters in the entertainment field. They've assigned a young woman, a junior associate, to work on my contracts, and I already like her. She's current, yet very knowledgeable. She's already made a lot of calls on my behalf, and I get the sense that she's going to be a tough negotiator," Torie answered, grateful for the change in subject.

"That sounds terrific, honey, but have you thought about this? Are you sure you want to go with a female? I mean, you know how this business is. Maybe a man might be more beneficial to you," Brenda said.

Torie sighed beneath her breath, amazed at her mother's perfected ability to put a negative spin on any subject. As she thought of a response that would put her caring but pessimistic mother at ease, a slow smile came to her face while her mind recalled the image of the tall, dark and scrumptious man she'd shared an elevator ride with that morning.

"What? What are you smiling about?" Brenda asked suspiciously.

"Nothing, I was just thinking about the fact that Cooper & Beardsley is home to more than its fair share of fine male attorneys. I should bring you with me the next time I go there and hook you up with one of those professional men, Mama." Torie laughed.

"Me? Child, please. You know I'm not even studying no man. All that's over with for me," Brenda said.

"Mama, why do you say things like that? You're a beautiful woman, and you've got a lot to offer a man. If you'd stop acting like you have one foot in the grave, you could—"

"Torie, I don't want to talk about this again. Like I said, I am not interested in offering anybody anything. And just because you're taking a very wise and necessary break from men right now, does not mean you should be concentrating on my personal life. Hook me up? Please. You just focus on your career and nothing else, you hear?"

"Yes, ma'am," Torie said with another exaggerated under-the-breath sigh.

Torie was seven years old when her parents split up for the last time. It had been a tumultuous relationship, plagued by the resentment born of unfulfilled dreams. The couple had had one more child, a son they named Darius, but that wasn't enough to save the relationship. Darius was still a toddler when their father moved, first out of the home and then out of Georgia. He eventually ended up in California, where he remarried. After that, they saw less and less of him, and she watched as her mother grew more and more disinterested in romance altogether.

"Come on, Mama, let's go do some shopping," Torie said, purposely changing the subject.

"There are still quite a few stores that I can't let you leave New York without hitting up."

The women spent the afternoon trying on shoes and clothes at a variety of trendy boutiques. At various times, when each believed the other to be preoccupied with a dress or a pair of boots, they would get lost in their private thoughts. The faraway look that clouded Brenda's eyes as she thought of herself on yesterday's stages was matched by the one in Torie's eyes as she dreamed of passionate kisses with a gorgeous man in a red tie.

Chapter 3

Trapped

Monte dropped his PDA into the pocket of his briefcase as he moved past the vacant reception desk and toward the bank of elevators. He glanced at the Movado watch on his left wrist and issued a mild curse beneath his breath. He was late and the boys would already be in bed by the time he got home. He hated not being home for dinner and detested missing the opportunity to tuck them in after a few rounds of XterminatoR video game on the PS3 system. The fact that tonight's holdup couldn't be avoided due to a delayed international flight of one of his most prominent clients and a very long meeting did not make him feel any better.

Monte rubbed his forehead, glad that it was Friday night and he could look forward to a relaxing weekend with his sons. Tomorrow morning he planned to take them to the lake for the day where they'd get the canoe out if the weather was good and maybe do some fishing. He stepped into the elevator, pressed the button for the lobby and leaned back against side wall. The doors began to close, but they stopped just before they met when a slender hand slid between them.

Monte looked, startled to see that the hand belonged to none other than Torie Turner.

"Ooh, I made it," she said, moving into the elevator with a small hop.

Monte quickly depressed the open button until Torie was completely inside.

"Thank you." She smiled.

"You're welcome." Monte smiled back.

Torie reached out and pressed the already-illuminated lobby button. The doors closed and the elevator began its descent. Torie stared at the buttons, fully aware of Monte's eyes on her. From her peripheral she could see him studying her, and while an intense look like his should have made her nervous or uncomfortable, it didn't. She refused, however, to allow herself to turn to meet his gaze, despite the fact that his eyes felt like magnets, drawing her own eyes to his.

Monte started to speak. He cleared his throat, parted his lips and the lights went out. The elevator lurched to a stop, propelling Torie into Monte.

"Oh," she screamed.

"What the—" Monte began.

He caught Torie in one arm and steadied her.

"Are you okay?"

"Yeah…yes. Whoa, that was scary. What's happening?" she asked, her voice tinged with panic.

"I don't know," Monte answered. He reached out, fumbling with the buttons in an attempt to press the now-blackened one for the lobby. The elevator remained motionless and dark. He felt along the smooth panel again until he located the alarm. He pressed that button and the shrill sound rang out, causing Torie, who was still standing very close to Monte, to jump even closer.

"It's okay. I'm just ringing the alarm to alert someone that we're in here," Monte said.

The rich timbre of Monte's voice had an almost calming effect on Torie. Almost, because although it was a well-guarded secret, Torie was deeply afraid of the dark.

"Shouldn't an emergency light come on or something?" she asked.

"You would think so, but I'm guessing maybe the power is out. I'm sure it'll come on in a few minutes."

"Do you really think so?"

"Yeah, I'm sure of it. This is a state-of-the-art building and we're constantly having elevator inspections and such. And even if it doesn't come on, the lobby security will respond to the alarm," Monte said.

He said these words even though he really wasn't sure of any of it. But making others feel at ease in any situation was in Monte's nature and it was a talent at which he was very good. It was what made him a loving father and son, and a superb lawyer. He could feel the anxiety radiating off of Torie, and the last thing they needed while trapped and suspended twenty-odd stories off of the ground was for her to get hysterical.

"Okay," came Torie's measured reply.

She accepted Monte's rationale and allowed it to sink into her mind and racing heart. Of course he was right. This was, after all, the Time Warner building, located in the center of midtown Manhattan on a Friday night. This building and its personnel was equipped to deal with this type of emergency, and it would just be a matter of minutes before they were rescued. Torie inhaled a deep breath. She closed her eyes and allowed her muscles to relax. As her pulse slowed and the queasy feeling in her stomach began to subside, she became aware of how close to Monte she was still standing after having been thrown into him. Although she could not see his face and could only make out the outline of his form, her other senses kicked in, drawing her into his presence. She felt the warmth of his body next to hers and the scent of him, a mixture of maleness and a heady aftershave toyed with her sense of smell. She suddenly felt wobbly again and reached out for him. Her hand found his strong forearm, and she clenched it.

"Maybe we should sit down," Monte said, interpreting her move as a sign that she was unsteady on her feet, perhaps near fainting.

He quickly removed his suit jacket and laid it on the floor beside him. He felt for Torie's elbow and then slowly guided her to the floor and onto his jacket. He slid down the wall beside her, loosening the knot in his tie. Monte stretched his long legs out in front of him and let out the deep sigh that he'd been holding in.

"This really sucks, doesn't it?" Torie asked.

"Well, I guess you could say that it's not my idea of how to spend a Friday night." Monte chuckled.

He thought for a moment about his boys and his mother, who were at home in bed for sure. Cheryl, the nanny who looked after them while he worked, would probably call the office soon, to see how much longer he would be delayed. She'd have given his mother her sleeping pill and made sure the guardrails on her bed were in place. He'd had the bars installed a few months ago when his mother had either rolled off the bed or fallen while trying to get up. She'd broken her wrist when she'd hit the floor and now he made sure that she was secure in bed every night. Cheryl would begin to get worried soon and would then call both his cell and car phones. Monte felt around in the dark until he found his briefcase. He reached into the side pocket and retrieved his PDA.

"Humph, just like I thought. No signal," he said.

All the device was able to provide was a sliver of light from the small screen when he depressed the power button.

"And then there was light," Monte joked.

He lay the device onto his lap and let his head roll back against the elevator wall.

"So what would you be doing tonight if you weren't trapped in this elevator?" Monte asked.

"Me? Uh, I'd probably be home, curled up on the sofa by now," Torie answered.

"Yeah, right. On a Friday night in New York City? Come on, for real. What would you be doing?"

"I'm serious," Torie cried. "I'd be watching *20/20* or whatever's on right now. Ooh, and tonight was the season finale of *NCIS,* too. Shoot."

"Listen to you, sounding like a regular couch potato." Monte laughed.

"And what's wrong with that? I happen to have a very nice couch, I'll have you know," Torie said over Monte's raucous laughter. "What's so funny?"

"Nothing, nothing. I'm sorry," Monte said, putting his laughter in check. "It's just that I can't really picture you with curlers in your hair, flannel pajamas and a big bowl of popcorn," Monte said, chuckling.

"You know, if you're going to make fun of me, you could at least introduce yourself first."

"Monte…Monte Lewis. I'd shake your hand, but I'm not sure where it is," Monte said.

"It's nice to meet you, Monte Lewis. I'm Torie…Turner."

"I know who you are," Monte responded.

"Oh?"

"We, uh, actually shared an elevator a couple of weeks ago. You were coming up to the office to see Monica Schwartz. You're an actress, right?"

"Yes, that's right. Don't tell me you've seen my work?" Torie asked.

Monte realized at that moment that he could lie and say, yes, he had. He could tell her that she was a terrific actress and possibly score big points with her, but that wasn't his style. He believed that when you start off telling one lie all you're doing is setting yourself up for a dozen more lies to follow.

"No, I can't say that I have. What have you done?"

In the darkness, Torie's smile broadened. She hated when she met people who, immediately upon learning that she was an actress, pretended to recognize her. Someday she was certain that she would be a face that people knew immediately, but that day was not here yet. Torie Turner's was not an ego that needed to be stroked with false praise. She found Monte's honesty refreshing.

"Well, let's see. There was that mouthwash commercial last winter. Then there was the Reynolds Wrap foil spot around the holidays. And my personal favorite, the genital herpes medicine gig." Torie laughed. "Pretty impressive résumé, huh?"

"I guess I don't watch much TV," Monte said apologetically.

"I'm just teasing; that's not all I've done. There have also been a couple of small theater productions in Atlanta and in Philadelphia. But all that is about to change."

"Change is good," Monte said.

Several minutes of silence ensued before either spoke again. Monte was reminded of his first date with Shawna and how comfortable he'd felt with her, as though they'd already known each other for a lifetime. That same sense of familiarity had come over him now, and he secretly thanked whatever higher power had orchestrated this dilemma for him.

"Is it getting warm in here to you?" Torie asked suddenly.

She didn't wait for an answer before unbuttoning the top two buttons of her blouse and removing the lightweight leather jacket she wore. She knew that her nerves were shot, which probably attributed to the warm flush that had invaded her flesh.

"Yeah, definitely warm," Monte said, removing his tie altogether.

"So, Monte, what fun and exciting evening are you missing out on?" she wanted to know.

Monte talked animatedly about his sons and their weekend plans. Without offering much detail, he told Torie that since becoming a single parent, he dedicated his weekends to activities with his boys and found their outings to be the perfect break from work and the other demands of life. Surprised and intrigued by this revelation, she asked how he managed to care for two boys on his own and he told her that his boys had a middle-aged woman named Cheryl, who was the best nanny, cook and housekeeper in the world, caring for them. She wanted to ask about the boys' mother, but she didn't want to be obvious.

Hours passed as they opened up about their respective childhoods, sharing stories of playground mishaps and adolescent insecurities. Torie laughed raucously at Monte's jokes, vulnerable to his understated yet undeniable sense of humor. Their conversation had its serious moments when Monte shared his concerns over his mother, who was ailing, and Torie talked about the hole created in her life by her father's absence. However, those moments were cathartic for both of them, as they felt unexplainably comfortable sharing such intimacies in the secluded space of their private bubble. After being caught up in a cozy tête-à-tête, it was finally Monte's growling stomach that reminded them both that they hadn't eaten since midday. Monte reached into his right pants pocket.

"All I've got is a half pack of Doublemint gum. How about you?"

Torie sifted through her Dooney and Bourke giraffe print.

"I've got a few orange-flavored Tic Tacs mints and I think... yes, here it is. A half a roll of Mentos candies," she exclaimed excitedly.

Despite his efforts to keep Torie calm, Monte had begun to grow uneasy himself. There had been no contact from security and it seemed as if no one knew that they were trapped in the elevator. He began to consider the possibility of them running out of air, but quickly chided himself for being silly. That was probably the last thing that could happen to them.

"We're going to starve to death," Monte said half-jokingly.

"No, we'll probably get dehydrated first. It takes the human body about thirty days to starve after the cells feed off of one another," Torie answered.

"That's encouraging." Monte chuckled.

"Sorry. Here," Torie said, offering Monte a handful of chewy peppermint Mentos candy.

Their fingers bumped as Torie placed the candy in his hand. The contact sent a charge through Monte as it had done every time their shoulders or sides had touched over the past couple of hours. He liked being near her, listening to the softness of her voice when she spoke or the sound of her breathing when they were silent.

They polished off the candies in minutes and their hunger seemed to be cranked up a notch in spite of it.

"Well, at least we'll have fresh breath while our bodies dry out." Torie laughed.

Her face was turned toward his and he felt a burst of minty air hit his cheek. On impulse, he angled toward her, leaning forward until he was inches away from her. She did not move away, nor did she speak. His stomach muscles contracted and he held his breath. The next move was his, and his heart raced at the thought of kissing that beautiful mouth and having her respond in kind.

He hesitated, all sorts of thoughts running through his mind. There was always the possibility that his advance would be unwanted. Yet, the urge was too compelling for Monte to back away from it. He brushed his lips lightly across Torie's mouth and the quivering in his stomach only intensified. He covered her lips and, to his surprise, she parted to receive him, allowing his tongue to melt into the softness of her candy-coated mouth. She leaned her body into his, and he slid his arm around her torso, securing her against him. Monte had not allowed himself to think about how much he missed the feel of a woman in his arms, but suddenly he was overwhelmed with a sense of longing for feminine suppleness. If he had not known it before, this moment confirmed for him the fact that it was a woman's touch that made him feel most like a man.

Monte shifted his weight, drawing Torie closer to him. A soft purr escaped from her lips and was lost inside of his mouth. He reached out in the darkness, his hand finding her shoulder. He rubbed through the material of her blouse and wished that he could touch her skin. Instinctively, he knew that it was soft, covering toned limbs. He moved his hand up to her face, running two fingers along the line of her cheekbone. His hand slid to the nape of her neck and caressed silky hair. He gently pushed her head closer to him, wanting to devour her.

"Mmm," he breathed, trying to recapture his senses, but failing.

Monte knew that he was going too far, but it had been so long since he'd felt such an intense arousal and wanting. Torie Turner had captured his attention from the first moment that he inhaled her scent and laid eyes on her. Yet, tonight, trapped for what seemed like an eternity in the oppressive, closed space of an elevator, he'd found himself enraptured by more than her physical beauty. Unable to see more than a faint outline of her, he'd felt his heart stroked by the sound of her melodic voice and his spirit touched by the sincerity of her personality. He'd learned in those hours that Torie's beauty was far more than skin-deep. Not since his late wife had he clamored like a fiend just to hear every word a woman had to say. He knew that now that he'd been given the opportunity to be an audience to Torie's thoughts, he would never be the same again.

Monte struggled with himself, trying to find the strength to disengage from the web he and Torie had spun. His arousal was undeniable, bordering on painful. His fingers, having developed a mind of their own, found the buttons of her blouse and deftly opened first one and then another. The fabric of the lace bra she wore teased his fingers. His tongue probed deeper and hers explored him just as eagerly. When he squeezed the fleshy mound of her left breast, Monte felt as if he'd fallen off a cliff, with no hopes of finding his way back to firm ground. And just when he thought that he would be lost in her sweetness forever, the spell was broken. The lights came on and the elevator jerked a couple of times before resuming its descent as if it had never been stalled.

"We're saved," Torie said breathlessly, her hand automatically moving to her open blouse.

She looked into Monte's eyes and smiled. A nervous chuckle from Torie prompted one from Monte, as well.

"Here, let me help you up," he said as the elevator neared the lobby level.

Monte rose and grasped Torie's hand in his, pulling her to her feet. He held on to her hand for an extended moment, gave it a strong squeeze and released it just as the doors opened. They were greeted by two building security guards.

"Sir, ma'am, are you okay?"

"Yes, we're fine. What happened?" Monte asked, retrieving his rumpled suit jacket from the floor.

"There was a blackout—most of the city and parts of Westchester were out. We contacted the fire department and let them know that we had an elevator alarm going off, but they said they'd only be able to respond to emergencies."

"I guess two people trapped in an elevator, suspended in midair for hours, doesn't qualify as an emergency, huh?" Torie huffed.

She snatched her leather jacket from the floor and slipped her arms into it, obviously ticked off.

"You definitely haven't been a New Yorker very long!" Monte laughed at her teasingly.

"I'm sorry, ma'am," one of the security guards said. "We really wanted to get you guys some help. We kept trying to talk to you over the intercom, but they were out, too. So sorry about this, folks."

The guards were clearly upset, feeling a personal failure at not having been able to help them.

"Hey, guys, we're out now, and I'd say no worse for the wear," Monte said, throwing a meaningful glance at Torie, who blushed noticeably. "Thanks for all of your efforts, guys."

Monte shook both of the men's hands. They both smiled, grateful for Monte's graciousness despite the evening's distress. Torie thanked them, as well, assuring the men that she did not hold them responsible for the situation.

"Ms. Turner, can I give you a lift home?" Monte asked.

The spell that Torie had cast over him had remained intact, even after the power came back on and they'd emerged from their metal nest. Monte looked into Torie's eyes, hoping to convey to her what he was feeling, even as he struggled with exactly what those feelings were himself. He wanted to spend more time with her. After all they'd divulged to each other, there was still so much he wanted to know about her and so much that he wanted to share. With the taste of her lips still lingering on his own, Monte could not erase the feel of her womanly frame in his arms. He wanted to reclaim those arousing sensations and take them to even greater heights.

"No, no...I'm sure you want to get home yourself...check on your boys. I'll just hail a taxi," Torie said.

Even as she said no, Torie felt a loud and resounding *yes* pounding inside her brain. She could feel herself being pulled to Monte, and although what had transpired between them shocked her, she wanted more of it. She had never in her life been so open and unguarded with a man she'd just met, but there was something about Monte that made it difficult to be guarded in his presence. The racing of her heart and the pulsing in the center of her womanhood had yet to taper off, and her head told her that the logical thing to do would be to put some distance between herself and the seductive Monte Lewis before she did something that she would later regret.

Monte studied her face for a moment, and he thought he could see a flash of conflict reflected in her beautiful eyes. It was enough to place his desire in check.

"You're right—I really do need to get on home. Cheryl is probably beside herself with worry. Come on, I'll hail a cab for you."

The pair stood out on the sidewalk in silence, each lost in complicated thoughts. The air was warm for April, yet Torie hugged both arms around her body. When Monte was at last successful in stopping a yellow taxicab for her, she slid quickly into the passenger seat, but turned to face him before the door closed.

"Thanks for everything tonight, Monte. I don't know what I would have done if I'd been in that elevator alone," Torie said.

"I can safely say the same thing," Monte said, smiling warmly.

"Good night."

Monte pushed the door closed and watched the taxi peel away from the curb. He stayed where he was, standing until the red taillights blended in with all the other cars headed in the same direction. Finally, he pulled his PDA from his briefcase to call home and headed toward the building's underground parking lot to retrieve his car. Even as they moved in opposite directions, both Monte's and Torie's thoughts remained in an elevator of the Time Warner building. The kiss they'd shared played an equal role in their revelries, as did the quiet admissions made in the dark. They'd reached a level of intimacy with each other that some people were still searching for after several dates and a night full of passionate sex. Each was left with the conclusion that people ought to spend more time trapped alone in elevators.

Chapter 4

The Scent of Roses

On the Monday morning following the blackout, Monte arrived at his office at noon, having spent the morning at the boys' pediatrician's office for their annual checkups. He always subconsciously breathed a sigh of relief whenever his boys went to the doctors, as he was no stranger to unexpected illness. Both Joshua and Josiah were progressing as they should and neither one had so much as a bump to complain about. For Monte, that was all the news he needed to have a good day. Little did he know that there was even more ahead to be happy about.

"Morning, Mr. Lewis. Looks like your day is off to a bright start." His secretary, Margaret, beamed as he leaned over her desk to retrieve his mail.

Perplexed by Margaret's unusual greeting, Monte's eyebrows came together in a question mark. Margaret simply smiled and pointed toward the open door of Monte's office. He moved cautiously toward the office, glancing back at Margaret, who continued watching him with a look reminiscent of a cat that'd eaten a canary.

In the center of Monte's desk rested a large bouquet of

yellow roses. Their scent had already filled the spacious room and their vibrant color seemed to provide more illumination than the florescent lights overhead. Monte was even more mystified as he plucked the small card from the vase. In a delicate, beautiful penmanship, there was a simple message that read, *It was a pleasure sharing an extended elevator ride with you. Monte Lewis, you are a lifesaver. Torie T.*

Monte looked down at the flowers again and noticed that tied to the large satin yellow-and-white bow in front of the vase was a pack of assorted Mentos. He burst out laughing, his robust voice ringing throughout his office and out into the corridor where Margaret still sat beaming.

"Told you," she called.

Monte pulled back the leather office chair behind his desk and sat down. He stared at the flowers for several minutes, inhaling their scent. He tore the package of Mentos open and popped one into his mouth, before closing his eyes and taking another deep breath. The memories that he'd spent the entire weekend fighting to suppress came rushing back, heating him up inside. He opened his eyes and read Torie's card again and again. Her handwriting was as delicate and graceful as she was.

Over the past two days Monte had convinced himself that what had happened in that elevator between he and Torie was a simple case of two people being forced together during a stressful situation. He'd told himself that a woman as electrifying and breathtaking as she had to be a lot more complicated than she'd appeared, and complications were the last thing he needed in his life. He'd spent the past three years focusing on his boys and helping them cope with the loss of their mother. He'd pushed all of his own desires and longings aside, striving to fill the void left by Shawna as best as he could. When his mother's health had taken a turn for the worse last year, he knew that he'd made the right decision and dedicated himself even more to taking care of his family. Those hours spent with Torie in that elevator had stirred up long-buried feelings and, since then, Monte had managed to push them back down where they belonged. Yet, even as he'd done that, he knew that he was telling himself a lie and had been all along.

Monte was startled from his deep thoughts by a quick rap on the open door to his office. In walked Brent Stolzberg, a colleague, as well as his racquetball partner and friend.

"Monte, my man, what's cooking?" Brent asked as he walked in.

Brent took at seat in front of Monte's desk. Motioning to the flowers, he said, "Whoa, what's this?"

"Man, you wouldn't believe it if I told you," Monte replied.

He spent the next few minutes explaining to Brent how he'd been trapped in the elevator with one of the firm's newest clients last Friday night and how afraid she'd been. He left out the part about the passionate kiss they'd shared and also didn't mention how she'd been plaguing his thoughts ever since.

"And she sent you flowers to thank you for holding her hand through the ordeal? Wow, classy lady. What's her name?"

"Torie Turner."

"Oh, this just gets better and better. *The* infamous Torie Turner? I've heard that she's a ten on the knockout scale," Brent said. "All the single guys around here are practically drooling over her…and some of the married ones, for that matter, too."

"Okay, so we're rating our clients now? Boy, if that's not a clear indication that we definitely don't have enough to do around here, I don't know what is," Monte replied.

"Come on, Monte. Don't tell me you've never checked out a client before. Even a monk like you can acknowledge a good-looking woman when you see one," Brent retorted.

"Whatever. Look, Torie Turner is, indeed, a beautiful woman. Happy?"

"Not yet. Not until you tell me what went on while you two were trapped in that elevator all of that time?"

"Nothing. We talked. I kept reassuring her that everything would be okay. Eventually, we got out, I hailed a taxi for her and that's it."

"Yeah, right. And that's why she sent you this hundred-dollar bouquet of roses? Get real, Monte."

"I'm serious, that's it. I don't know what you want me to say, Brent."

"I want you to say that you're going to call Ms. Turner, thank her for the flowers and then ask her out to dinner or a show."

"Why on earth would I do that?"

"Are you serious? Monte, there are about a million reasons why you should do that, starting with the fact that you haven't been out on what qualifies as a date in years and ending with the fact that Torie Turner is a beautiful woman who appears to be interested in you."

"Interested in me? What? No, you're reading this all wrong," Monte said nervously. He paused for a minute, glancing at the flowers. "What makes you think she's interested in me?"

"Duh! Jeez, Monte, has it been that long? Let me school you, my naive friend. Women don't send flowers to men just because," Brent answered.

"The flowers are a thank-you for keeping her calm in the elevator. That's all."

"I'm sure she said thank-you when you got out of the elevator. Those flowers are about ten percent *thank-you* and ninety percent *I want to get to know you better,*" Brent said.

Monte thought about Brent's words, considering their undeniable merit. She had said thank-you, repeatedly. There was no real need for her to send the flowers, unless she was interested. But, on the other hand, maybe that was just the type of person she was—gracious and overly demonstrative. Either way, Monte reasoned, he had already made up his mind.

"You know what, Brent? It really doesn't matter why she sent the flowers. I'm not interested in dating Torie Turner," Monte said definitively.

"Why not?"

"Why not?"

"Is there an echo in here? Why not?" Brent asked again.

"Because—"

"Because you've taken this ridiculous vow of celibacy and solitude that makes absolutely no sense. That's why," Brent said.

"Brent, you don't know what you're talking about," Monte said. He pulled his lips in tightly, a sign that he was growing increasingly uncomfortable with the direction of the conversation.

"Monte, I love you like a stepbrother, but it's time you got honest—if not with me, at least with yourself. Shawna would not want you living this way," Brent said softly.

Monte was poised to get defensive and tell Brent that he really had no idea what he was talking about. He wanted to tell his friend to back off, but something stopped him. He leaned back in his seat and his eyes gravitated to the left, toward the credenza behind him. There was a picture of Shawna, the boys and him, taken about six months before she died.

"She'd give you permission to be happy if she could," Brent added.

"What makes you think I'm not happy?" Monte asked, lifting the framed photograph from the shelf.

"I'm not saying you're not happy. I know you love the boys, and for some crazy reason you even love this place. I'm just saying that you're blessed, man, but all that's missing is someone to share it with."

"I'm blessed? Listen to you sounding like a *brotha*. Keep on hanging out with me and you're going to get your white-boy card revoked," Monte joked.

"See there, now your memory is fading. I already became an honorary *brotha* last Thanksgiving when your mom got me hooked on her collard greens and black-eyed peas," Brent replied with a laugh. "On that note, I've got a meeting to get to. Just think about what I said and, after you do that, invite the woman to a harmless lunch."

"Later, man," was Monte's noncommittal reply.

Left alone with his thoughts, Monte stared at the photo of his family. He couldn't believe that he still loved Shawna as much as he did the day he'd married her, but there it was, sitting in the middle of his chest like a boulder. A love that once lifted him and made him believe he could fly now weighed him down and left him feeling like a drowning man. For the first few months after her death, he'd looked up to the heavens and asked over and over again why she'd left him. He never got a response so eventually he stopped asking. He'd heard that when people lost a loved one, they often felt that person's presence, comforting them. He didn't feel that. All that Shawna's death had left was a hole that he'd believed could never be filled. Suddenly, a thought occurred to him that perhaps what Shawna had really left was a space and not a hole. Maybe she'd left that space purposely so that there would be room in his heart for someone new to love.

Monte spontaneously turned toward his computer. He struck a few keys on the keyboard and pulled up the firm's client directory. Within seconds, Torie Turner's name, address and telephone number appeared on the screen. He picked up the handset on his telephone, punched her digits into the keypad and waited. Her recorded voice came on after the second ring, urging him to leave a message.

"Hello, Torie. This is Monte…Monte Lewis. I just, uh,

wanted to say thank-you for the flowers. A beautiful yet entirely unnecessary gesture, but you are more than welcome. Listen, I was wondering if you'd like to, uh, have lunch sometime. I know your schedule is probably pretty hectic, but if you have a free hour or whatever, give me a call. Okay, well, take care."

Monte hung up and expelled the breath he hadn't even realized he'd been holding. Uncertain as to if she'd call or how that would make him feel, Monte allowed the alluring scent of Torie's roses to soothe him temporarily. He couldn't deny that she'd touched him in a place that he'd thought no one would ever be able to reach again. He certainly hadn't been looking for it, but it was precisely because he wasn't looking that she'd appeared. While he was a man who'd long ago stopped believing in destiny and fate, he could not help but wonder if Torie Turner had come into his life and his elevator at precisely the moment when he needed her to.

Chapter 5

Cards on the Table

"So, Ms. Turner, have you hung out in any nice elevators lately?" Monte asked.

They were seated at an intimate table for two at an obscure Italian restaurant in walking distance of the Time Warner building.

"Ha-ha. Very funny, Mr. Lewis," Torie replied.

Monte beamed beneath the warmth of her sunny smile.

"I'm just teasing you. How've you been?"

"I've been well, thank you. And for the record, I've been avoiding elevators ever since," Torie answered.

Monte ordered a cabernet sauvignon by the bottle when the waiter approached. When Torie had returned his call, he was crushed to know that she was actually in California on business. She returned his hopes when she informed that she'd be back in town in a couple of days and would love to have lunch with him. They made plans to meet on Friday, two weeks after their fateful night together. For the days leading up to their date, Monte found himself wafting between moments of elation and others of despair. He didn't want to make too much of her acceptance of his invitation, yet he couldn't help but think that it meant, as Brent stated, that she was interested in him. Seated across the table from her now, he felt like a goofy teenager, unsure of himself.

Torie gratefully accepted the glass of wine poured by the waiter. She took a protracted sip, quenching her dry throat. She chided herself silently, annoyed at how nervous she was, seated across from Monte. That morning, with their date looming before her, she'd changed her outfit three times before finally deciding on a long-sleeved animal-print blouse and white slacks. She wore minimal makeup as usual, opting for a subtle shimmer on her eyes and a tinted lip gloss. She wore her shoulder-length bronze-copper hair pulled back from her face and held in place by a silver comb. Confident in her appearance, Torie wished that some of that confidence would calm the butterflies that were flitting around in her belly.

"I've got to tell you, those flowers you sent me caused quite a stir around the office," Monte said.

"Really? Why is that?" Torie asked.

"Well, it's not every day that I get elaborate floral arrangements from a female."

"Oh? So do you usually get them from a male?"

"That's cute. Okay, I guess I set myself up for that one. What I meant to say was that it was an unusual sight and people were curious," Monte said.

"Were they interested in who they were from or what you did to deserve them?" Torie asked.

"Both."

"What'd you tell them?"

"Absolutely nothing. I figured I'd keep them guessing."

"I see. Well, next time, maybe I'll send you some balloons, instead. All right?" Torie laughed.

"Definitely all right…especially that part about next time," Monte said.

His meaning was not lost on Torie. She took another sip of

wine and smiled at him. It was so difficult not to be captivated by everything about Monte—his eyes and his smile drew her in like a spider's web. She'd wanted to resist him and the feelings he had ignited in her, but denying herself the pleasure of the company of a man like Monte proved more difficult than she had imagined it would be. When she'd set her mind to avoiding romantic entanglements for the foreseeable future, she had not encountered the likes of Monte Lewis. There was a calm that surrounded the man like a cloak, traveled with him and pervaded the mood of anyone who came into contact with him. She liked the way she felt around him, and going against her previous stance did not seem like such a high price to pay to enjoy that feeling.

"Can I ask you a question?" Monte asked.

"You just did."

"Wow, are you sure you're an actress and not a comedienne?" Monte retorted.

"I'm sorry." Torie laughed. "I have this bad habit of cracking jokes when I'm nervous."

"What do you have to be nervous about?" Monte asked.

His surprise was evident on his face as he regarded her. The notion that the beautiful, poised woman seated across the table from him would be nervous in his presence or that of any man, for that matter, was absurd.

"You, Mr. Lewis. For some reason, you make me nervous," Torie admitted shyly.

"I assure you, Torie, you have nothing to be nervous about. I'm harmless."

"Somehow I doubt that, but we digress. You wanted to ask me a question. Shoot."

"Well, it's actually twofold…my question. And excuse me in advance if this is out of line or inappropriate, but I'm a little out of practice at this. I was just wondering if you're seeing anyone and, if not, if, uh, if you'd like to see me. I mean, you know, maybe go out from time to time—schedules permitting—to dinner, a movie, or whatever you're into."

There, he'd said it. Monte could almost feel his throat closing up as he waited for her response. He hadn't meant to be so blunt, especially not before they'd even ordered their meals. However, he could not continue to deny how alluring he found her and he needed to know early on if there was even a chance that they could see each other again. He told himself that knowing up-front would set the tone for the remainder of their lunch date, and he could avoid getting his hopes up if this was a one-shot deal.

"I like you, too, Monte," was Torie's simple reply.

Monte held his breath, unsure if a *but* was about to come. When she said nothing further, he surged ahead for her.

"But?"

"But nothing. You like me and I like you, too. It's out there now. So, why don't we just sit back, enjoy our lunch and see what happens."

Damn, he thought, *what style.* No one could deny that this woman had panache. He took her advice and enjoyed every minute with her that afternoon. They chatted more about her upbringing in her hometown—North Atlanta, Georgia—in comparison to his as a native New Yorker. They discovered a few things they had in common, such as both being raised in single-parent homes and neither of them having a relationship with their fathers. Monte was an only child; Torie's younger brother, Darius, was a deputy sheriff back in Atlanta. They laughed when they discovered that they'd both served as senior class presidents in their respective high schools, and while Monte had played the tuba in the school band, Torie tooted the clarinet.

Two hours later they emerged from the restaurant, with sides that ached from laughing. Monte's hand rested on the small of Torie's back as they strolled down the street. He deposited Torie in front of an entrance to the subway so that she could catch a train to her Upper East Side apartment. As they prepared to part company, Monte leaned in, kissing her lips briefly. He'd been aching to taste her mouth again all through lunch and flushed at the feel of her lips against his. With a tentative pledge to get together again soon, they moved away. Monte whistled as he made his way back to the office and his good cheer certainly had everything to do with the sexy woman who'd brought a smile both to his face and to his heart.

Chapter 6

Undress My Heart

"Monica, that's terrific. That's exactly what I was hoping to hear from you today," Torie squealed.

She leaned forward in the passenger seat of Monte's Lexus ES350 luxury sedan and slapped the open palm of her right hand on her thigh. She turned to Monte, her face a bright beam of happiness, which served to bring out a smile on his face, although he had no idea what she was so happy about.

"And they're ready to sign?" Torie asked. "Wonderful. Okay, uh, sometime next month? Okay, I'll wait to hear from you. Thank you again, Monica. Take care."

Torie disconnected the call and dropped her PDA onto her lap. She clapped her hands together three times rapidly before covering her face with her hands.

"Are you going to tell me what we're celebrating or am I going to have to guess?" Monte asked.

"Oh, my goodness, Monte. It's unbelievable. No, scratch that. It is totally believable because I'm damned good at what I do," Torie stated emphatically.

"Yes, you are. Now, what are we talking about?" Monte asked again.

"Well, a few weeks ago, I read for a lead spot in a new series pilot called *Higher Learning*—I know, same title as that nineties movie with Ice Cube. It's a drama based on a college campus. I read for the role of Senora Phelps, head of the recruiting department. It's a really great role...one that leaves a lot of room for growth. I had a good feeling when I read but, you know, you never can tell. Anyway, it turns out that feeling was right on the money!" Torie shouted.

"You got the part?" Monte asked.

"Not only did I get the part, but Monica said they're offering me a very sweet deal to boot. She'll have the written contract next month, and she says I'll be pleased."

"Damn, girl, that's all right! Congratulations. Look at you—been in the Big Apple for five minutes and you're already doing great things. Go 'head, Ms. Turner," Monte shouted, his enthusiasm paralleling hers.

"Oh, Monte. I can't even tell you what this feels like. I mean, it's one thing to strive for something and envision it for yourself, but when it actually happens, it's surreal. I don't know what I did to be so blessed, but I'm truly grateful."

"What you did was to be beautiful, talented, smart and driven. That's a lethal combination, by any measure," Monte said. "Don't you want to call your mom?"

By this, their third date, Torie had already shared with Monte a bit of her relationship with her mother. She'd told him how demanding her mother could be, and she'd admitted that while her mother had always been her biggest supporter, there were times when her mother's visions for Torie's future conflicted with her own. At those times the pressure that Torie felt could be overwhelming as she struggled to follow her own course, despite how tenaciously Brenda tried to steer her into another direction.

"I'll call her...later. Right now I just want to savor the moment, you know. I know there is an urge when good things happen to us to run right out and shout it to the world, but some things—like this one—are just so big that you need to keep it private for a while and soak it in," Torie said.

They drove in silence for a few long moments. Monte's excitement for Torie's good news was another in a list of indicators that he'd had over the past couple of weeks, telling him how caught up he was with her. It almost felt as if her success was his own and he didn't think he could have been any happier if, in fact, it *were* his own.

"I'm happy I'm here with you in your big moment," Monte said, breaking the silence.

Torie turned to face him, while Monte kept his eyes on the road ahead of them.

"I'm glad you are, too," Torie said sincerely.

They drove the remaining few miles in relative silence, save an occasional comment on the scenery around them. It was early on Saturday and they were headed out to the lake house in Ronkonkoma, about an hour's drive from where Monte lived in Sands Point. Monte had bought the lake house just a few months after Shawna died. Their house had so many memories that he'd thought that having a change of scenery on the weekends would be good for the boys. It turned out that he was right. Being able to do activities like fishing and going out on the lake in a canoe brought smiles back to his boys' faces and to his own. For the first year after Shawna died, they'd drive out almost every Friday night and stay through Sunday evening. It was a place of solace and comfort and, Monte felt, one of the best investments he'd ever made.

Now that his mother was living with them, Monte and the boys only went out to the house a couple of times a month, usually when his mother was feeling up to going with them. Otherwise, Cheryl would stay in Sands Point and look after her. Today, Monte's hope was that he and Torie could spend some time alone, away from crowded restaurants and other people. He couldn't deny that he found himself in a constant state of arousal every minute he spent with her. Today, if the mood was right and if Torie was feeling half of what he was feeling, he hoped they would fulfill every one of their desires.

Monte gave Torie the grand tour of the small cottage-style house and the surrounding grounds. The two-bedroom home was modestly decorated, with fireplaces in the living room and the master bedroom, two bathrooms and a fully loaded kitchen. Out behind the house there was a barbecue pit and screened patio, and the yard area was surrounded by a thicket of trees and shrubbery that offered privacy from the next house several hundred yards away. He took Torie down to the lake, which was a short walk from the house. They sat beneath a tree, looking out at the water for a while, easy chatter flowing between them. When they returned to the house, Monte spread a blanket in the backyard and left Torie out there reading a magazine while he prepared the brunch he'd packed for them.

"Wow, don't even tell me you cooked all of this yourself," Torie exclaimed when Monte spread the food in front of her.

"That depends. What do I get if I say yes?"

"Mmm, how about I kiss the cook," Torie said, licking deviled egg from her fingers.

"Promises, promises."

They ate and talked some more about Torie's new role, a topic that made Torie's light eyes shine even more brightly than they did.

"When you were a little girl, was acting the dream you held for yourself?" Monte wanted to know.

"I was seven when I decided that I wanted to act. I remember telling my mother that I thought the most powerful people in the world were people who could make others laugh, cry, be happy or sad, just with a few words or a smile. She thought I was just being what she liked to call my usual dramatic little self, but I was serious. I never wanted any other career."

"So you're doing what you love. Isn't that the best feeling in the world?"

Torie lay back on the blanket, staring up at the sky for a moment before answering. She searched for the words to describe how she felt. Monte lay beside her and held her hand.

"It is. It's acting out a fairy tale," she answered at last. "What about you? Did you always want to be a lawyer?"

"Nah, I wanted to be a pilot. I thought I'd go into the air force, learn how to navigate planes and eventually end up in space operations."

"Wow, space? Don't tell me you wanted to walk on the moon?"

"I hadn't really thought that far, but, hey, you never know. But I quickly realized that I didn't want to end up in a war so the air force was probably not the best way to avoid that. Besides, my mom was always dropping hints about how nice it would be to have a lawyer in the family." Monte smiled.

He rose up on one elbow so that he could peer down into Torie's face.

"Oh, don't I know about that mother pressure," Torie exclaimed, rolling her eyes.

"Yeah, but it actually turned out to be a good thing for me. I went to law school, absolutely fell in love with the field and, voilà, here I am."

"Here you are," Torie replied, staring into Monte's eyes.

Monte glided two fingers down the side of Torie's cheek, amazed at the softness of her skin.

"Tell me about your father."

"There's not much to tell. I guess I don't even remember

him, at least not much other than what my mother told me," Monte mused.

"Do you know if you look like him?"

"Yeah, I look exactly like him. It's funny because sometimes you hear that when a woman and man split up and that man leaves their child or children behind, the mother can take her anger out on the poor kid. It's especially bad when the kid looks like the father. But not *my* mother. My mother always told me how handsome I was, how much she loved me. Even though my father left her to struggle on her own, she held his little boy close, looked in a face that was the spitting image of his father's and loved him," Monte finished wistfully.

"That's beautiful." Torie smiled. "I bet that's why you're such a great dad."

"How do you know what kind of father I am?"

"Well, because every time you talk about one of your sons, there's this dreamy proud-papa look that comes into your eyes. And you smile at the mere mention of their names. And you work hard, for them." Torie paused. "And you've helped them go on through what has to be the worst thing that can happen to a little boy."

Torie reached up and touched the side of Monte's face. He turned his face to kiss the palm of her hand.

"I find your patriarchy incredibly sexy, Mr. Lewis."

The way she looked up at him, her gaze a mixture of seduction and timidity, made his heart flutter with equal strength as in his loins. His lips found hers and an immediate electric bolt shot through him, causing his senses to sing. Their kiss was slow and probing, neither of them felt the need to rush. They wanted to savor each moment, as if by doing so they could lock the seconds of pleasure into their memories forever.

Monte's tongue slid deliberately over Torie's, intertwined with it in a sexy waltz without music. She sucked on his bottom lip as if trying to extract its very essence and nibbled at his top lip, making a sensual meal out of him. Monte's breathing sped up as he grew more aroused. He could feel the blood rushing to his manhood and, try as he might to slow the tempo of his sexual longing down, he was powerless to ebb the flow of the current that was propelling him forward. Suddenly, he broke the connection of their lips, leaning back slightly to look at Torie's angelic face.

"Are you okay…with this?" he asked.

"Better than okay," Torie answered as she moved her hand to the back of Monte's head and let her fingers roam through the thick curly hair. "You are quite the kisser, Mr. Lewis."

"You're not half-bad yourself." Monte smiled.

He planted a small peck on Torie's lips.

"Have I told you how absolutely breathtaking this place is?" Torie said.

"*You* are absolutely breathtaking, Torie Turner," Monte replied.

Torie's smile radiated from her eyes. The perfection of the day seemed almost too good to be true. If one of her girlfriends were telling her this story, she would caution her that she was moving too fast. She would say that three weeks was nowhere near enough time to get to know a man and that her friend was being caught up in a lust that was clouding her judgment. However, she would only be looking from the outside, and from that vantage point there was no way to understand what happens when two souls connect on the basest level. The past three weeks had been free from pretention or game playing. They had not allowed anyone or anything from the outside to interfere with or influence their courtship and, as a result, they had been free to be entirely open and honest about their attraction to each other. Torie did not feel that they were moving too quickly, and while she didn't join him at the lake with the intention of moving their relationship to the next level sexually, it was beginning to feel as though that were the next logical place for them to go.

"I want you, Torie," Monte said, as if reading her mind.

Torie searched his eyes and it was clear that he felt the magnetic pull as strongly as she did. It was a force that was greater than both of them and far more evolved than pure lust. Torie kissed Monte firmly on the lips, hoping to convey what she didn't trust words to express.

"Baby," Monte said softly but firmly, "these past few weeks have been amazing. I…I didn't expect this. I wasn't looking for anyone, but there you appeared. I feel like you came into my life at the precise moment you did for a reason. I believed that I could make a happy life for myself, my boys and my mother and be satisfied with that. But, Torie, you've made me realize that there's a part of me that's been unsatisfied and unhappy."

"Monte, I don't know what to say. This feels too good to be true," Torie whispered.

"You don't have to say anything. I know it's too early to think about what's going to happen in the future, and I don't care about that at this moment. All I know is that, right here, right now, this is all that matters."

Monte stopped talking, as if all the words that had poured out of him had left him exhausted. He searched for an escape from the frenzy of emotions that were racing through him, but there was no such escape.

"Torie, I've been alone for a long time. To be honest, I think I was preparing myself to spend the rest of my life alone. I feel like a big kid, unsure and clumsy."

"I think that's another thing that's so endearing about you, Monte. The fact that I'm not just another notch on a very long belt for an incredibly gorgeous man," Torie replied.

"I'm not a ladies' man, Torie, but I'm still a man and I

want…well, I want to feel like a whole man again. I want to feel that with you," Monte said.

Without waiting for a reply, Monte kissed Torie's eyelids, one at a time, staying the tears that had begun to form in them. She had never felt this close to a man in all of her thirty years, and she recognized that the bond she felt for Monte was beyond sex and far ahead of reason. It was spiritual in nature and, she realized, that was a more powerful aphrodisiac than any other.

Monte's hand moved to Torie's tight torso. He pushed the orange tank she wore up, exposing a flat stomach. He let his hand roam and felt her stomach muscles constrict under his touch. He moved up farther, finding soft mounds of flesh that rose and fell beneath his hand. He sought to free her breasts from the lace bra. Once freed, her nipples responded to his touch, standing taut at attention. He bent his head, his lips making contact with the ripe buds one at a time. Torie moaned, spurring Monte on. He licked her nipples, encircling them with just the tip of his tongue. Torie writhed beneath him, arching her back so that her breasts were thrust farther into his face. He read her body language, understanding that she needed more, and he complied. Monte took one breast into his large mouth, devouring it, dining on it. He sucked with all his might, allowing his tongue to lap at the nipple alternately. With his thumb he flicked at the other nipple, not wanting any part of her to feel neglected. Monte took his time with her breasts, almost as though he would be perfectly content with just tasting those perfect peaks all day and night.

Torie lifted her leg, encircling Monte's massive thigh and rubbing it up and down against him. She reached behind him, her hand landing on his muscled rear. Through his khaki shorts she squeezed and kneaded that strapping bulge of muscle and flesh. Monte sat up, pulling Torie upward with him. In a sitting position, he pulled the tank over her head and then slid her bra straps down. He unhooked the clasp from the back of the laced material and, when Torie's torso was completely bare, Monte stared in admiration. To him, she was pure perfection. He breathed heavily, before leaning forward to kiss each of her shoulders in turn. He found her mouth again to continue the dance their tongues had begun earlier.

"Monte," Torie whispered, her mouth moving to his left ear.

Monte thought that his name had never sounded sweeter than it did as it tumbled from her tender lips. She slid her tongue into his ear and he trembled. She nibbled at his earlobe and he thought that he would pass out from the sheer pleasure of it.

Torie stopped tonguing Monte's ear abruptly, disengaging from his embrace. He opened his eyes, alarm coating his handsome face.

"Take off your shirt," Torie said, the tone of her voice revealing the depth of her arousal.

Monte complied without hesitation, pulling his T-shirt over his head roughly and tossing it away from him. Torie smiled as she let her eyes roam freely across his sculpted chest and abdomen. She rose and Monte watched in a daze as she moved slowly around him until she was standing behind him. When she placed her fingertips on his shoulders, he felt as if he had been waiting for her to touch him there all of his life. She began to knead the tight expanse of neck and shoulders firmly, which felt better than a massage at any overpriced salon Monte had ever experienced. But when he felt Torie's tongue lapping between his shoulder blades, he knew he'd never visit another masseuse again.

"Ooh," he groaned between clenched teeth.

Torie's hands slid to Monte's pectorals as she dropped to her knees behind him. As she encircled the hard flatness of his nipples, he couldn't tell if it was the sensations from her fingertips or the feel of her lovely bare breasts pressing into his back that caused his erection to intensify. He didn't care what it was, as long as he could extend the pleasure forever. Monte turned slightly, grabbing Torie's arm forcefully and pushing her down onto the blanket all in one swift movement. He covered her mouth, taking her kiss with force and stealing her breath away. Torie raised her arms above her head in surrender and Monte grabbed both of her hands in his, holding her immobile as he ravished her mouth, face and neck with an eager tongue.

From a distance Monte heard the sharp tone of a trumpet blaring, and he thought that it was the perfect accompaniment to the symphony they were creating. When the sound grew louder, Monte realized with a start that it was his cell phone ringing.

"Ignore it," Torie whispered into his ear.

And Monte did, at first. But the tones continued and he realized that he could not simply ignore it. He was a man with a family.

"Hold on a minute, baby," he said, disengaging from Torie.

He snatched the device from the top of the picnic basket where he'd left it. Torie's impatient expression made Monte want to chuck the phone into the lake and get back to loving her.

"Hello," he said, without looking at the display. "Cheryl? Cheryl, what's wrong? I can't hear you."

Monte sprung to his feet, moving a step or two closer to the cabin in the hopes of receiving better reception.

"Is he talking? Is he awake? Okay. Yes…yes. Where are they taking him? Okay. Ask Mrs. Thompson across the street if she can stay with my mother and Joshua. I'll meet you there. Okay, Cheryl. Thank you," Monte said.

He turned toward Torie, who sat looking up at him, her eyebrows knotted and a question poised on her lips. She had wrapped her arms around her naked breasts.

"Baby, I'm sorry—we've got to go. It's my son...Josiah," Monte said as he hastily began to throw the remnants of their picnic lunch back into the basket.

"What happened?" Torie asked, jumping to her feet.

Her call fell on deaf ears as Monte the lover took a backseat to Monte the father.

Chapter 7

A Father's Love

Torie picked up her bra and quickly slid into it. By the time she'd pulled her shirt over her head, Monte had snatched the blanket off the ground, tucked it under an arm, picked up the basket and was heading toward the cabin.

"He fell off of his bicycle and hit his head on a tree stump. Cheryl said he lost consciousness and there was a lot of bleeding. The ambulance is taking him to North Shore University Hospital," Monte said.

He tossed the contents of his arms into the cabin, turned off the lights and shut the door behind him. He quickly locked it, engaged the alarm and strode toward the car, with Torie trotting to keep up with him. They jumped into the car, spitting gravel beneath the wheels as Monte took off with warp speed.

It took them about forty-five minutes to reach the hospital, during which they traveled in relative silence. Torie attempted to reassure Monte, telling him several times how tough kids were and that she was certain that Josiah would be fine. She could tell that Monte was tortured by the distance and time it was taking to get to his son, and she wanted nothing more than to make him feel better. However, she could tell by the grunts he offered in response to her statements of reassurance that he was not in the mood to be comforted.

They pulled into a parking space just outside of the emergency-room department and Monte sprang from the car. Torie followed, uncertain as to whether she should just wait in the car or trail behind him.

"I'm Monte Lewis. My son, Josiah Lewis, seven years old, is here," Monte said breathlessly to the first nurse he saw at the triage window.

"Yes, Mr. Lewis. Right this way," the nurse responded.

Torie lagged behind, watching Monte disappear behind the swinging doors of the patient area without a glance back. Torie stood for a few moments, looking around at the handful of other people in the waiting area. Finally, she slid onto one of the yellow plastic chairs that lined the room's wall and waited. As the seconds ticked by, Torie tried to focus on the news program that was playing on the thirty-two-inch television mounted in one corner of the room, but it was a task that proved too difficult. Her mind could not help but replay the day as she thought about how it had neared perfection.

From the good news she'd received from her lawyer to the confidences she'd shared with Monte and, finally, to the lovemaking they had embarked on. It had the potential to be the best sexual experience she'd ever had, of this she was certain. Yet, it was ruined because Monte had responsibilities that far surpassed anything he felt or had with her. She understood that. Torie was not that selfish of a woman that she could not respect the fact that Monte had two children and an ailing mother who depended on him. It was admirable that he was managing to raise his children, care for his mother and still maintain his successful position at a prestigious law firm. However, it was the very thing that she admired about him that made her come to the reluctant realization that she would not and could never be the most important thing in Monte's life.

That insight was startling to Torie, causing the blood in her veins to suddenly feel cool, sending a chill up and down her spine. She had begun to feel extremely close to Monte. From that evening spent in the elevator, where he'd made her feel less like she was suspended in midair in what could be a death trap and more like she was floating on a magic carpet, to today, Torie had continuously let her guard down with Monte. He'd gotten into places that she'd rarely allowed anyone access and he'd been equally as forthcoming with her. Yet, there was a part of Monte's life that she feared was a space where she was and would always be an outsider. She could never fill the place held by his dead wife, not with him or his children. What's more, she did not relish the thought of becoming a stepmother.

Torie's thoughts were interrupted by the sound of her name being called. She looked up to find Monte standing just outside of the swinging doors. Torie stood quickly, crossing the room in a heartbeat.

"How is your son?" she asked.

"He's fine. He's fine. A little banged up, but my boy is tough," Monte said.

"Oh, thank God, Monte."

Monte reached out and pulled Torie into his arms. They hugged for several extended seconds and, once again, Torie felt the connection between them, thick and warm like a blanket that shielded them. Yet, she knew that the outside world was waiting. She pulled back and looked into Monte's eyes. She saw how the worry and uncertainty of the past ninety minutes had left an imprint on his handsome face, making him look less like the sexy suitor she'd come to know and more like a dutiful parent.

"The doctors are going to keep him overnight, just to be on the safe side, but all of the tests they've run look great."

"I'm so glad to hear that, Monte." Torie smiled.

"Do you want to come in and meet him?" Monte asked.

Torie wavered in one awkward moment. Part of her wanted to say yes and go inside to meet one of the most important people in Monte's life. Yet, there was an equally persuasive part of her that said no, this was not the time. She didn't know if there ever would be the right time.

"No, he's had enough for one day. Why don't you go ahead back in there to him. I'm sure he just wants his daddy right now," Torie said.

"Are you sure?"

Torie rubbed the outsides of Monte's strong forearms, wishing she could just fold herself up inside of his arms again and remain there.

"Yes, I'm sure. Go ahead. I'm going to head back into the city," she said. "Unless you need me to do anything. How's your mother and Joshua?"

"They're fine. My mother's been responding well to the new medicine she's on. She's even been up and about the house a little bit. Cheryl's going to spend the night at the house with them while I'm here with Josiah. Sure you don't want to stay at the house with them?"

"No, I'm going to catch a train home. Just call me if you need anything, okay?" Torie smiled.

"All right. But here," Monte said, reaching into his front pants pocket and retrieving his car key. "Take my car."

"No, Monte, I can't take your car. How will you and Josiah get home tomorrow?"

"We can catch a taxi. I don't live far from here. I still have my...the car Shawna drove is in my garage. I'll make arrangements to get my car from you later on. No big deal."

"Are you sure?"

"Of course. I just feel so bad about getting you all the way out here on the island and then—"

"Nonsense, Monte. You had no way of knowing this would happen," Torie said.

Monte walked Torie out to the parking lot. Inside his Lexus, he set the navigation system so that she would have door-to-door instruction to get her back to her apartment in Manhattan. Monte lingered for a moment, feeling torn between his desire to be with her and the necessity of being with his son. It was Torie who finally nudged him to return to his son's bedside.

"I should get going before it grows dark. Give me a call tomorrow when you get Josiah back at home, okay?" she asked.

"Sure thing," Monte said. He kissed Torie briefly before climbing out of the car and shutting the passenger-side door. He leaned in through the open window.

"Can I ask you something?" Monte paused.

"Sure. What's up?"

"Did you have a good time…before…at the lake?"

"I had a *fantastic* time," Torie responded, a slow smile spreading across her face.

Monte's face opened up, and for the first time since he'd gotten the call about Josiah, he looked exactly like the sexy man she'd fallen for in that elevator.

"Maybe we can do it again sometime—I mean, without the hospital and all this," Monte said softly.

Torie touched his chin, her smile telling him all that he needed to hear.

"Thank you for being so understanding. It means a lot to me," he said.

"No thanks necessary. Try to get some rest tonight," Torie replied.

She put the car in reverse and Monte backed away to the curb. He stood and watched her pull out of the lot. As he made his way back inside to his son, Monte felt a significant peacefulness brought on by the belief that for the first time in three years he had someone to share his trials and triumphs. Torie had, in a very short time, come to be a special part of his life and he intended to do nothing but nurture their relationship and happily watch it grow.

Chapter 8

In Too Deep

"I don't know, Lisette. I feel so turned around right now. I mean, a couple of months ago, I was certain that all I wanted to do was focus on my career. I hadn't dated in months and I was actually enjoying my alone time. Now, I find myself daydreaming about Monte instead of focusing on the scripts in front of me or studying the tons of acting guides I've bought," Torie said. She poured another glass of merlot and leaned back into the cushion of her sofa.

Three weeks had passed since their day at the lake, and she and Monte had only managed to see each other twice in that time. First, they grabbed a brief lunch together when Monte came into the city to pick up his car a few days after Josiah's injury and then Torie accompanied Monte to a New York Bar Association dinner party at the Park Avenue Hotel. It was a lovely affair and Monte looked so scrumptious in his tuxedo that Torie had a hard time concentrating on the dinner and the exchange of pleasantries with the other attendees. She'd had an early flight to catch the following morning to attend her brother's graduate school commencement exercises in Atlanta. By the time she returned to New York two days later, Monte was off to Dallas for client meetings that carried into the next week. To say that Torie missed Monte was an understatement.

As she sat in her living room with her best friend since college, Lisette Vargas, she gave voice to the nagging doubts that had been troubling her incessantly.

"*Chica,* listen. I don't know why you always have to make things so black-and-white. You've told me nothing but great things about this guy and now it's, like, you think you can't have it all…the banging man and the popping career," Lisette said.

"That's because usually when people have it all, something happens. Lisette, you of all people know what can happen when I try to have it all," Torie said.

The allusion she was making was not lost on Lisette. After all, she was the one who had held Torie's hand last year when she'd given up one of the biggest opportunities of her career because her then-fiancé, Kevin, had begged her to follow him to Spain where he played professional basketball. Unfortunately, they were only there for three months before Torie caught Kevin in a ménage à trois with two Spanish cheerleaders.

"You cannot count that idiot as having it all. You loved him, Torie, and you did what a woman in love does. You trusted him and put your faith in him. I mean, yeah, you had to learn the hard way that he was an untrustworthy SOB, but you learned."

"You're right. I did learn, but it cost me. Dearly. I won't ever let that happen again."

"And you shouldn't. But what does that have to do with Monte? He's right here, in New York City, with you. He's an entertainment lawyer so he understands the industry you're in. He's established, got his own money—girl, he sounds like all that and then some."

Lisette had been a broadcast journalism student at the University of Georgia where Torie studied theater arts, and from the moment they'd met, Torie was convinced that Lisette should have been a drama major instead. Lisette was today forging a fabulous career for herself as a special news reporter for a popular cable station. Somehow, she managed to always find the time to be there to counsel her friend when she needed it. In fact, it was Lisette who convinced her to move to New York after her breakup with Kevin and she'd been there through all the tears and *why me's?*

"You're leaving out the part about the ready-made family. I don't know if I'm capable of all this. Just when I land the role I've been working toward since college, I find someone who I could see myself spending the rest of my life with. How am I going to balance both?" Torie took a sip of wine. "Maybe I'm being greedy to even try," she concluded.

"That's complete nonsense. There are lots of successful actresses who have it all. Look at Jada and Will Smith. He had a kid already when they got together. And…and how about that guy…that comedian you like? He had two kids by what's-her-name when he hooked up with his second wife and they've been together for years."

"True, but obviously those women wanted to be mothers… stepmothers, whatever. Point is, I don't even know if I want to have kids. On top of that, Monte's boys are seven and nine years old and, unlike your examples, they are not the product of a divorce. Their mother died, Lisette, and they've been dealing with that loss for the past three years. Who's to say they even want me to come into their lives?"

"Well, my little worrywart, there's only one way to find out the answers to all of your questions," Lisette said, chugging the remnants of her glass back dramatically.

"And what's that?"

"Just jump in and let the currents take you where they might."

Torie allowed Lisette's advice to settle between them as she silently sipped her drink. Torie didn't know how to adequately express her feelings about Monte and his children to Lisette without coming off sounding selfish. She wanted Monte, there was no doubt about that. Despite her well-laid plans to focus on her career and take a break from men, she found herself longing for his touch, his taste and his presence. He'd stirred her soul like a master chef and that was not something she could just walk away from. However, Monte was a package deal. He came with two little human beings attached to his hips, and that was an unexpected twist to an otherwise enticing road.

Chapter 9

Hesitant Heart

Torie had reviewed the contract with Knight Productions to shoot the pilot and six episodes of *Higher Learning* earlier in the day and she was in the mood to celebrate. She could think of no one else she wanted to celebrate her success with other than Monte. She was relieved when he accepted her offer of a candlelight dinner for two at her apartment. She spent the afternoon shopping for ingredients for a fresh vegetable salad, a turkey lasagna that was to die for and a key lime pie that would blow his socks off.

When the doorbell rang at seven o'clock sharp, Torie had just put the finishing touches on dinner. She checked her hair in the full-length mirror on the back of her bedroom door, smoothed the form-fitting dress she wore and took a deep breath in an effort to calm the excitement that had her feeling buzzed. She greeted Monte at the door with a warm kiss and a tight hug.

"Whoa, girl, I almost forgot how good you look," Monte said.

Once inside the apartment, he pulled her back into his arms and squeezed her body against his. His mouth found hers, and it was obvious from the heat of his kiss that he'd missed her just as much as she'd missed him.

"You're wearing my favorite tie," Torie remarked when they came up for air.

She smoothed the red tie around Monte's neck; it was the same tie he'd been wearing the first time she'd ever laid eyes on him.

"And you're wearing my favorite smile, beautiful," Monte said.

"Come in and have a seat," Torie said.

She took Monte by the hand and led him into the living room. Monte removed his suit jacket and sat down on the overstuffed sofa. He glanced around the room, immediately taken by the coziness of it. This room was the perfect reflection of Torie's personality—it was tasteful, not overdone and full of interesting little fixtures. There were small African sculptures and crystal figurines on the frosted-glass shelves that hung from one wall. There was a deep oak entertainment center against another wall that housed a stereo system and dozens of books. The coffee table in the center of the room was made of wood and glass and in its center rested a colorful centerpiece of silk flowers and votive candles. The room smelled of a mixture of vanilla and sandalwood. Monte felt immediately relaxed. It had been a grueling day at the office, filled with contract negotiations and marathon phone calls. Two minutes of being in Torie's home, seated in its soothing embrace, was enough to erase the tension from his body. That was something he'd come to miss—coming into a home run by a woman. An image of Shawna hanging curtains in their living room when they first bought their home flashed through his mind suddenly. Although he had not changed anything significant since she'd passed away, the house no longer held the aura of a woman and, as such, had lost some of its powers to soothe.

Torie entered the living room, carrying two glasses of white wine.

"Here you go," she said handing one of the glasses to him. "Or would you prefer a beer? I've got Coors Light," she offered.

"No, this is just fine," he said.

Monte realized that it was more than just her home that made him feel so relaxed. It was Torie herself—her sexiness and her peaceful nature—that made him feel at ease.

"Long day?" she asked.

"Is it that obvious?"

"A little bit," Torie conceded.

"Yeah, I had a lot going on today. But I don't want to talk about that. How've you been?" Monte asked.

"Everything's great. Monica just finished reviewing the contracts. She made a few minor changes, which they've agreed to, and she wants me to come in to the office on Monday to go over everything and sign. After that, I'll get the scripts and rehearsals will get under way before long."

"Sounds like things are moving along just fine. But how are you?" Monte asked.

Torie smiled, once again caught off guard but at the same time pleased by Monte's innate habit of cutting through the surface issues and getting to the core of the person. This was one of Monte's most endearing qualities.

"I'm fine. I've got to admit, though, that I'm a little nervous. All this happiness feels like a little too much for one girl to hold," Torie said.

Monte placed a finger beneath her chin, raising her face slightly. He leaned forward and kissed her tenderly on the lips.

"Nonsense. You deserve all the happiness in the world and then some," he said.

Their kiss was full of promise. For his part, Monte felt

the pieces of himself coming together in that kiss. He had been waiting for weeks to feel her mouth against his again, to taste her juices and hold her in his arms. It had been too long, an agonizing accumulation of days and nights in which he actually felt a physical ache for her. It was ironic to him that he had gone years without a touching a woman, and now that he'd experienced the sensation again, he felt as though he could not do without it.

Torie relaxed against Monte as she felt fireworks explode inside her heart. She'd been craving his kiss, dreaming about it and reliving the moments they'd spent together at his lake house. She wanted to feel his body up against hers again and it was all she could do not to pull him down to the carpeted floor and beg him to take her right now. But she held back. She wanted tonight to be perfect. She was determined to let the night unfold at its own pace, slowly and deliciously, so that she could relish every moment of it.

The silence of the room as they kissed was interrupted by a low growl from Monte's stomach.

"Are you hungry?" Torie laughed.

Monte laughed with her, rubbing his midsection.

"You heard that? Well, I guess there's no point in me trying to pretend I'm not starving. I didn't eat lunch today," he admitted.

"Well, that will just not do. Come with me, Mr. Lewis. Let's get you fed and satisfied," Torie said, standing and grabbing Monte by the hand.

"Baby, you don't have to feed me food to satisfy me," Monte said as he stood.

He pulled Torie into his arms and began kissing her neck hungrily.

"There's plenty of time for that later. Right now, we need to get your stamina up. You're going to need it," Torie teased.

She led the way through the living room and into the small

dining room. The room was illuminated by four tapered candles in the center of the glass-and-wrought-iron table. There were two place settings on opposite sides of the table for four. Monte took a seat as instructed while Torie stepped into the kitchen. She returned moments later with two glass bowls of salad. She disappeared three more times, each time returning with another dish or accompaniment that made Monte's mouth water. When she finally took a seat across from him, Monte reached out, took her hand and offered a short grace in which he blessed the food and the beautiful hands that had prepared it.

There was not much conversation between them during the meal as Monte devoured the food. He had two hefty servings of lasagna and then finished what Torie had left on her plate. Torie suggested they take dessert and coffee into the living room.

"Girl, I don't think I can get up from here," Monte said, rubbing his full belly. "As a matter of fact, I know I can't. I'm just going to sit right here, stuffed in this chair, for the rest of the night." He chuckled.

"Suit yourself, but your dessert's going to be waiting in the living room," Torie said seductively.

Monte turned to watch her walk out of the room. The tight roundness of her ample behind swaying in the fitted dress she was wearing caused an immediate constriction of his blood vessels. It didn't take but a second for him to pull himself out of the chair to follow. He didn't really care what she was carrying in the dish in her hands. He wanted something else for dessert.

Torie turned the radio on to a smooth jazz station while they sipped coffee with dessert. There was a comfortable silence between them while they nibbled, their hunger building by the second. It wasn't long before Monte felt as if he was going to literally crawl out of his skin if he didn't touch Torie again.

He dipped a finger into the whipped cream she'd doled on top of his slice of pie. As he moved toward her face, she opened her mouth in anticipation. When the cool cream touched her tongue, she closed her mouth around Monte's finger and sucked. Monte replaced his finger with his tongue, pulling Torie on top of him. His hands found their way to the treasure he'd been eyeing all evening, cupping the firm mounds of her backside and squeezing.

"Torie," he sighed as she began tonguing his earlobe and neck. "Torie...I've been waiting for this."

"Me, too, baby," she breathed back.

"I want to see you," Monte demanded. "Take off your clothes."

Torie looked at him for a moment, before raising her body off of him and standing on her feet. Monte sat up, his eyes full of eager anticipation. Torie reached behind her and undid the zipper at the back of her dress. She used her right hand to pull the material away from her left shoulder. When she'd freed the right shoulder, the dress began to slip down her body. She placed both hands on her hips and slipped the dress down to her legs.

"Damn," Monte breathed heavily.

The sight of Torie's body was mind-blowing. The skimpy white lace bra and thong she wore served as an accent to glowing skin and sexy curves. Fully clothed, Torie was a beautiful woman, but looking at her bare essence from head to toe was more appealing than Monte could have imagined. He crawled from the couch to the floor on his knees, stopping before her. Cupping her bare behind, he pushed her forward, his face meeting the warmth of her center with zest. He inhaled deeply, the womanly scent of her tantalizing his senses. The strip of material was barely enough to cover her womanhood, which was unadorned by hair. He moved the fabric aside with his finger, exposing a tantalizing jewel.

The bursts of air that escaped him as he breathed caused a pleasurable shiver to run through Torie and she grabbed the back of his head, arching her body into him. Her desire to be tasted was the only thing she could focus on and Monte had what she needed in answer to that.

Monte nuzzled her with his nose, kissed her pert point gently at first. He introduced a hot tongue, bathing the outer lips with a tender stroke while squeezing her rear firmly. Torie's moans grew deeper, her gasps losing all delicacy as they escaped her throat. The sensuous music she made spurred Monte on and he dove in with a passion that surprised even him. While he sucked her tight bud he used two fingers to stir her inside, his tongue and fingers meeting and separating in a delicious rhythm.

"Ooh, right...right there," she breathed.

"There? Is this what you want, baby?" Monte asked.

"Mmm-hmm, yes...Monte!"

Torie's legs began to shake, threatening to give out beneath her. Reluctant to stop but determined not to let anything interfere with his efforts to please her until she begged for him to stop, Monte rose, scooping Torie off her feet and into his arms. He carried her into the bedroom and spread her scorching body onto cool cotton sheets. Torie watched as Monte removed his clothing slowly. Despite the eager anticipation on both parts, neither of them wanted to rush the experience. Joining their bodies was but a symbolic representation of how their souls had already been linked, and Monte aimed to show Torie just how much she had come to mean to him.

When Monte tossed a twelve-pack of condoms on the bed next to Torie, she laughed out loud.

"Humph, you don't think you're going to last that long, do you?" she said as she reached up for him.

Torie closed her fingers around Monte's neck, pulling his

face down to hers. She tasted herself on his lips, smelled her scent mingling with his and wanted to scream with pleasure. His first touch, as he glided his hands up the length of her thighs, sent a shiver through Torie's body. Torie reached between them, seeking and finding proof of his desire. She massaged him slowly, her hand moving up and down his rod with agility.

"I want to take you in my mouth," she breathed heavily.

"No," Monte refused her, knowing that he would not be able to hold out for more than a few seconds of being loved by her beautiful lips and tongue. "I'm still hungry," he said.

Monte slid farther down on the bed, positioning his face between Torie's toned thighs. From this vantage point, her vulnerable exposure to him was tormenting and provocative. His tongue found home again and, this time, she was free to thrash and thrust as much as she wanted to on the safety of the mattress. Monte became a man on a mission, his one-track mind focused on loving her body with all he had inside of him.

"Monte," Torie breathed heavily. "Please…oh, Monte, please stop," she cried out.

It was the cue he was waiting for. She pulled at him, grasping his shoulders, her nails digging into his flesh. She wanted more and he had so much more to give her. He moved on top of her, his mouth finding hers again. He settled in between her legs, which were parted to receive him. The wetness that greeted his hardness was a mixture of her moisture and his saliva, and it was a very warm and wonderful welcome. He moved against her, careful not to penetrate as he wanted to savor every moment for as long as possible. Torie pressed herself up against him, crying out at the luscious sensations that rippled through her body as their sexes made contact, while Monte bit his tongue to stop his own cries of pleasure.

Their foreplay carried on for what seemed like ages and until finally neither Monte nor Torie could wait another moment for completion. Monte quickly tore into a condom package and slid it onto his throbbing pole. Separated by nothing but a thin piece of latex, Monte penetrated Torie and, together, they rode wave after wave of pleasure.

"Torie, baby, you're so beautiful," Monte said as he stared into her eyes.

His release came sooner than he'd hoped, in an explosive rupture, and Torie held on to him tightly for the ride. When he was still, Torie slipped from beneath him and stumbled into the bathroom. Monte struggled to control his breathing as he heard her moving around. His eyes were closed when she returned to the bed and he fought to regain his strength. Torie rolled him onto his back and straddled his thighs. Monte's eyes jerked open when she covered his semistiffness with a warm washcloth. She wiped him down lovingly, before tossing the cloth aside and continuing to massage him with her hands. He responded to her touch, growing thicker with each passing second. This time, Torie did the honors of putting the protection in place, and when she was done, she slid down onto him, moving until he rested snugly within her walls.

"Do you have any idea what you're doing to me?" Monte asked in a growl.

"Do you want me to stop?" Torie teased.

"Never. I want you to do me until I pass out," Monte answered.

Torie rocked her hips slowly, moving back and forth, up and down like a snake. Monte's thrusts beneath her and his hands cupping her breasts made her feel more desired than she had ever felt in her life. The fine mist that had formed on their bodies turned into a sheen of sweat, a result of the physical workout they were putting each other through. When Torie increased the pace, bucking on top of Monte like a horse that needed to be broken, Monte grabbed her hips and held her in place so that she could feel every inch of him. Her climax was a like a dam breaking down, and she showered down on him, triggering his own release.

Torie collapsed against Monte, and he enveloped her in the crook of his arm. She rested her head against his chest. They lay in the coolness of the room for a long while in silence, allowing their elevated body heat to wane.

"Baby, I think it's time for you to meet my boys," Monte said softly.

He stroked the side of Torie's shoulder. She didn't respond right away, but continued to lay listening to the rhythm of his breathing. Her leg was thrown across his as they lay naked, the sheets and blankets nowhere to be found. It didn't matter because the heat they had just generated was enough to keep them warm in a blizzard.

"I don't know if that's such a good idea just yet," Torie said cautiously.

"What do you mean?" Monte asked.

"I don't know, Monte. I just think that maybe we should hold off on that for a while longer," Torie answered.

She knew this conversation was coming even before he brought the subject up. He had already made statements about how much she was going to love his boys and how he couldn't wait for them to meet her. It was just a matter of time before he came right out and asked her. She had practiced in her mind what she would say when the moment arose, but nothing she had come up with sounded right.

"Wait for what? Look, baby, I know you might be somewhat nervous about meeting them—boys can be a little rough and tumble sometimes—but I promise you, they're good kids."

"I'm sure they're great kids."

"So, what's the problem?" Monte said.

He shifted his body, sliding his arm from beneath Torie's body so that he could lean up on an elbow and look at her.

"There's no problem, Monte."

Torie tried to keep her voice light, sensing that she'd hit the sensitive area of Monte that she'd been trying to avoid.

"Well, then, you should come over and have Sunday dinner with us. My mother has been feeling a little better lately. She's been able to stay up a while longer and take a meal with us some days."

"Monte, I'm just not sure we're at the family-dinner stage. I mean, you and your boys have had a hard time. I'm sure seeing another woman in their home...seated at the same table their mother used to... I don't think it's the right time for me to—"

"Torie, that's nonsense. Yes, my boys have had a hard time but they're kids and they're resilient. They've adjusted to their mother's absence in their lives. They understand that she's no longer in pain and she's resting comfortably with God now."

"That's beautiful, Monte. But that doesn't mean you want them thinking you're trying to replace her in their lives."

"Of course not. Shawna will always be their mother, but they have room in their hearts for friends. Besides, I've told them about you and they can't wait to meet you."

"You've told them about me? What have you told them?"

"I just told them that you're beautiful, smart, funny and sweet. My oldest wanted to know if you were a *dime,* as the kids say. Of course I told him you were *all that.*" Monte laughed.

"You're crazy," Torie said, slapping Monte playfully on the chest.

"So it's settled, then?"

"No, Monte, it's not. Look, I just need a little more time. Can you give me that?" Torie asked.

She reached up and touched the side of Monte's face. She stroked it gently and, in doing so, hoped to soothe the disappointment he must have felt at her resistance to meeting his family. She didn't want him to press her because then she would be forced to reveal the doubts and misgivings she was having about the probability of their relationship being a long-lasting affair. Specifically, she didn't want to discuss her qualms about becoming a mother, especially not a stepmother.

Monte leaned in to kiss Torie.

"Of course I can give you that. It's cool. We'll wait until you're ready," Monte said.

"Are you sure you're okay with this?" Torie asked.

"Baby, as long as you keep putting that thang on me like you just did, I'm eating out of the palm of your hand. Anything you want, is yours," Monte said, shifting onto his back and pulling Torie on top of him.

There was little talking as night gave way to day and Monte and Torie continued pleasuring each other with heart, body and soul. They climbed a stairway to heaven, lifting each other to the highest of heights.

Chapter 10

Dear Mama

Monte drove slowly down the street, his tan Lexus moving at a speed of twenty miles per hour as he kept his eyes peeled for any sign of his ailing mother. It was just after sunrise and much of the neighborhood was still in shadow. He struggled to keep the feeling of panic that rested in his gut from rising to the surface. There was no time for panic, no time for him to fall apart. He had to find his mother before something happened to her.

He couldn't even believe that this had happened. He knew that his mother had been feeling much better. The symptoms of Alzheimer's disease seemed to be in recession, or at least had been laying dormant, he thought. His mother, Marva, had been even more lucid in the past few weeks, calling each of the boys and Monte by their correct names and remembering what they'd eaten for dinner the night before. Her doctors had said that she was responding well to the new medicines and that there was no reason to not expect that she wouldn't continue to be focused and coherent. As a result, Monte had stopped strapping his mother into her bed for fear that she would try to get up and wander around the house.

It was still dark when Monte, buried deep within his last hour of sleep, had heard a noise. He'd continued to sleep, though slightly disturbed, unwilling to give up the last vestiges of rest. He told himself that perhaps one of the boys had gotten up to go to the bathroom and that if there were something wrong, like an upset stomach or bad dream, either Josiah or Joshua would make their way to his king-size bed to wake him.

When Monte's clock went off, he was already awake, having never fully drifted back into sleep after he'd heard that noise. He got up immediately and traipsed into the master bath. After relieving himself and brushing his teeth, he headed down the hall to start the coffee brewing. He stopped in front of the boys' room, peered inside to find them still sound asleep. He moved farther down the hall and stopped in front of his mother's door. It was partly open, which was unusual. He remembered closing it securely before going to bed the night before. Monte pushed the door open and looked in. Marva was not in the bed. He stepped farther into the room and snapped on the light. He peeked behind the door and then moved toward the closet door. It was empty.

Monte hurriedly returned to the hallway where he checked the bathroom, the walk-in closet and finally the kitchen. There was no sign of her. The dead bolt to the basement door was still secure and the spare key was safe on top of the ledge above the door, far out of his mother's reach. He continued searching the house, flicking on lights everywhere he went. She was not in the dining room or in the family room. He returned to the hall and went into the boys' room. He shook Joshua, the eldest of his two sons, awake.

"Josh, did Grandma come in here this morning?" he asked.

"Huh? No, I...I don't think so," Joshua said, rubbing his eyes.

Monte moved to the window behind the boys' bunk bed that provided a view of the backyard. There was no sign of her there, either.

"What's wrong, Dad?" Joshua asked.

"Grandma's not in her room. I can't find her anywhere. I'm going to go out front and look around. Stay here," Monte ordered.

He controlled the tone of his voice, not wanting to alarm Joshua unless it was absolutely necessary. He went out to the front of the house and, as he reached up to disarm the alarm, he noticed that, instead of being red as it should be, the light indicating that the alarm was engaged was green. Monte roughly snatched the unlocked door open and ran out onto the front porch. He glanced up and down the driveway, before walking toward the garage. He punched in the code on the keypad next to the garage door and waited impatiently while it rose. All he found inside was his Lexus and Shawna's Nissan Altima sedan.

Back inside the house, Monte ran into his bedroom and slid into a pair of sweats and a T-shirt. He pushed his feet into a pair of Adidas flip-flops, snatched his wallet and car keys off the dresser and headed back out into the hall. He stopped in front of the boys' room, where Joshua was sitting up in bed, now wide-awake.

"Josh, I think Grandma went out walking somewhere. I'm going to look for her. I want you to call Cheryl and tell her what's going on. Ask her to come over early today. Then I want you to wake your brother up and you guys have a bowl of cereal. Okay, you got that?"

"Yes, Daddy," Joshua said, pushing back his covers and climbing out of bed.

Monte hurried out of the house and jumped into his car. He stuck the key in the ignition and, as the engine turned over, he closed his eyes and said a silent prayer, asking God to watch over his mother. He pulled out of the garage at such a high rate of speed that the tires screeched against the pavement.

Monte drove around for the better part of an hour. He called home from his car phone and, when Cheryl answered, he prayed that she had some good news for him.

"Is she there?" he breathed.

"No, Monte. There's no sign of her anywhere. I called Mrs. Anderson down the street...Estelle—you know, the lady she used to play bridge with? She said she hasn't seen her since Estelle came by here for a visit last week. The boys and I have searched the whole house. Monte, do you think we should call the police?"

"I'm going to the police station right now. Tell the boys to get ready for school. It's getting late," Monte said.

"Monte, they're dressed, but they've already said that they don't want to go. They're worried about their grandmother. Do you want me to tell them that they have to?"

Monte sighed, his eyes still scouring the sidewalks to the left and right of his car. The town was starting to come alive, and now that there were a few people out, he actually had to focus on each individual instead of just scanning for human figures.

"No, just let them stay there. I'll be back as soon as I can," Monte said. "And, Cheryl, tell the boys not to worry. I'm sure their grandma is just fine."

Monte added those words of reassurance without conviction, hoping that Cheryl could convey them in such a way that the boys would believe them. He didn't feel certain at all that his mother was okay and with each passing second the dread at all the possibilities began to take hold of him.

At the police station Monte was immediately taken in to see one of the detectives on duty. Because of Marva Lewis's advanced age and physical and mental conditions, there would be no waiting for twenty-four hours before filling out a missing-person's report. The detective took down all of her information from Monte and gave the photo Monte pulled from his wallet to the computer analyst to have scanned and routed to every patrol car's information screen. He had one of the patrolmen send it electronically to the local Kinko's copy center with instructions to be prepared to run color copies as soon as they got the word.

"Now, chances are we'll find your mother in the next hour or so. She can't have gotten very far on foot, especially at her age. However, if we haven't tracked her down by noon, I want you to call Robert Berger, the manager over at the Kinko's on Vine Street. Tell him that I told you to call and that he should run about one hundred copies off. Pick those up and start getting them posted around town. All right, Mr. Lewis?"

"Yes, Detective Smythe, that's not a problem. Is there anything else we can do?"

"As a matter of fact, yes, there is. I want you to head back to your house. I'm going to have a few officers come by directly to check out the premises. We just have to rule out any foul play."

"Foul play?" Monte said.

"Now, now, there's no need to panic. It's just the routine that we have to follow. They'll check out the house and the surrounding area. Just to be sure that your mother left on her own accord. Once they've done that, I want you to show them your mother's belongings and make sure that she hasn't taken anything with her—you know, a bag, her valuables or anything. Okay?"

Detective Smythe rose to his feet and Monte followed his lead.

"Is that it? Is that all I can do?"

"Yes, Mr. Lewis, that's all for now. I want you to try not to worry. Chances are your mother is sitting on a bench in a park or somewhere, taking a load off and enjoying the morning air. I'm almost certain of it."

Monte shook the detective's hand and headed back out to his car. The sickening sensation in the pit of his stomach had intensified and now he realized that the time to panic had arrived. His ailing mother, who was in the advanced stages of Alzheimer's was out wandering the streets. She was probably cold and alone, and, for all he knew, she could be hurt. He could kick himself for not getting out of bed when he heard that noise. And not securing the guardrails on her bed last night. How could he have been so stupid? He cursed his lack of intelligence.

Back at home, Monte worked overtime trying to keep the boys' fears at minimum. By nine o'clock, the police officers had gone through the house, inspecting the alarm system, the locks on the door and his mother's bedroom. They watched while Monte checked the clothing in her closet and drawers, as well as the jewelry that he kept locked in a safe in the hall closet. Nothing was missing, as far as he could tell. It appeared that she hadn't even put on her favorite sweater, which still draped the back of the natural-wood rocking chair in the corner of her room. She'd gone out of the house before dawn dressed only in her nightclothes and slippers.

At ten o'clock Cheryl and the boys sat down to do some reading. She told them that just because they'd skipped school for the day, there was no reason for them to think that they didn't need to exercise their minds a little bit. Monte squeezed Cheryl's shoulder in gratitude, thankful that she always seemed to know just what the boys needed and what he needed. Keeping Joshua and Josiah occupied for any length of time would help Monte focus on finding his mother.

Cheryl Amore had actually been hired by Monte's late wife, Shawna. She'd been recommended to Shawna when Josiah was a year and a half old and Shawna wanted to return to work. She'd been a stay-at-home mom since giving birth to Joshua two years prior to that and was looking forward to returning to her job as an insurance-plan administrator. The family Cheryl had been working for raved about this immigrant of Grenada who, at fifty years old, had raised two wonderful, successful sons of her own after being widowed ten years into her marriage and had worked with their autistic child until he was able to attend a full-day school program. Both Shawna and Monte fell in love with Cheryl's easy but no-nonsense mannerisms right away, and she immediately began helping to care for the Lewis's toddlers.

Monte knew that it was with Cheryl's support and dedication that he made it through those first few months after Shawna passed. He'd taken a leave of absence from the firm to be home with the boys, but was having a difficult time getting the then four- and six-year-olds to stick to any of the schedules Shawna had put in place. They were reluctant to sleep in their own beds, opting to set up shop in Monte's bed every night. They were temperamental and uncooperative with each other and Monte found himself constantly breaking up disagreements between them. It was not an easy time for any of them, but Cheryl helped them weather those stormy days and they came out on the other side a tighter group of man and young men. And then, just when things seemed to have settled into a new but acceptable normalcy, Monte's mother's health took a dramatic turn and necessitated Monte having to move her in with them. Once again, Cheryl did not miss a beat. Monte knew that he was fortunate to have her in their home and in their lives and he never missed an opportunity to let her know it.

"I'm going to drive around for a while. Call me on the cell or in the car if there's any news," Monte called out as he headed out of the door.

Inside his car, he checked his e-mail quickly on his

BlackBerry. He'd already sent his secretary a message, alerting her to a family emergency that would keep him at home for the day. She was instructed to clear his schedule and contact him only in an extreme emergency. He backed out of the driveway and punched in the speed-dial code set for Torie on his car phone. She answered on the second ring, and from the moment her voice filled the car, Monte felt a rush of faith that everything would be okay invade him.

"Morning, babe. Aren't you at the office yet?" Torie asked.

"No, I'm not going in today. I've got some trouble here," Monte said.

"What? Did something happen to one of the boys?" Torie asked, alarmed.

It was amazing how worried she'd started becoming over the boys. She was not used to the bumps and bruises, the constant spills and upsets, that happen in the lives of children, and the more time she spent with Monte, the more she realized that it took a strong constitution to get used to the unpredictable life a parent led.

"It's my mom," Monte replied.

He was headed toward the Sands Point Preserve, which was one of his mother's favorite places to go in the spring and summer months. When she was well, she used to walk the nature trails a couple of times a week with two other ladies from her church.

"Oh, no, what's wrong, Monte?"

The obvious concern in Torie's voice warmed Monte to his soul.

"I don't know. She's missing. I got up this morning and she was gone. It seems like she'd turned off the alarm and walked out the front door in her pajamas. The police are out looking for her and I'm driving around again. There's been no sign of her and …" Monte sighed. "I don't know what to think."

"Oh, God, Monte, I'm so sorry. Listen, I'm going to catch the Long Island Rail Road and come out to your house," Torie said.

"No, sweetheart, that's not necessary. The detectives said that there's really nothing we can do but wait. I just couldn't sit still, so I'm out driving around, hoping to see something," Monte said, pulling his car into a space near the park's entrance.

"Nonsense, Monte. It is necessary, and I'm coming. Just give me your home address. I can take a taxi from the railroad station," Torie said.

It was obvious to him that Torie would not take no for an answer. He quickly gave her his home address and the name of the stop on the train in his town, but instructed her to call him when she got to the station.

"All right, babe, I'm on my way. Just hang in there. I'm sure your mother will be found soon, and she's going to be just fine. Do you hear me?"

"I hear you. Thanks, Torie," Monte said.

Monte hung up the phone and stared out of the window toward the park in front of him. It took him several minutes before he got the strength to get out of the car. In those minutes, he thought about how people always complimented him on his strength and fortitude. So many people, especially men, believed that it is strength that makes a man. They never stop to think about where that strength comes from, as if a person is just born that way. Monte knew differently. He knew that his strength came from the women in his life, beginning with his mother, who nurtured him from birth, and continuing with every woman who'd ever guided, instructed, loved or taught him. He added Torie to that list of women, realizing that he was becoming more and more dependent on her. Just talking to Torie had the power to make Monte's days brighter, and touching her was like striking gold. As Monte sat in that car, he let himself acknowledge what he'd already known was there. He was in love with Torie Turner, and he knew that making her a permanent fixture in his life would be like winning a multi-million-dollar lottery jackpot.

Monte prayed that his family made it through this current ordeal intact. He especially prayed for his boys, not wanting them to have to suffer through any more loss in their young lives. They'd had enough. He told himself that after his mother was brought home safe and sound, he would make sure that Torie knew exactly how he felt and what his intentions toward her were.

Chapter 11

Lean on Me

At noon, Monte phoned Berger at Kinko's, and by the time Monte arrived at the copy center, Berger had two hundred copies of his mother's photograph printed, with the word *Missing* and the local police station's telephone number at the bottom. Two of the flyers were already posted in each of the windows of the Kinko's, and Berger had sent one hundred copies out with two of his young clerks to post and hand out to storekeepers in the town's business district.

"Mr. Berger, I can't thank you enough for that. How much do I owe you?" Monte wanted to know.

"I'll mail the invoice to your house. You can settle up later, after your mother's back home, safe and sound," Berger said.

He walked Monte out to his car, carrying the box of remaining flyers.

"Again, thank you for this. God bless you, man," Monte said.

"It's nothing," Berger said, waving Monte off. "I've got a mother, too."

Monte returned to the house to find the boys and Cheryl

at the table having sandwiches. Surprise stopped him in his tracks when his eyes landed on Torie, seated in the family room with the yellow pages on her lap, looking as beautiful as ever—and astonishingly comfortable.

"Okay, thank you very much for your help. And you have my number, right? Great. Thank you," Torie said into her cell phone.

She disconnected the call as Monte approached.

"That was the elementary school on Walnut Avenue. They're putting an alert out in the school and they're also sending an e-mail bulletin to the parents with a description of your mother. I read this article once about how elderly people who are suffering from Alzheimer's or any sort of dementia sometimes gravitate to places where children are, like schools or playgrounds. Studies on the subject are still inconclusive, but they think it has something to do with their memories of their own childhoods."

"What do you mean, like they're trying to go back to childhood?"

"I'm not sure. I was thinking more that they're struggling so hard right now, but they can go back and remember the most uncomplicated times of their lives. What do you think?"

Monte studied Torie's earnest face. He glanced at the notepad she had on the sofa next to her, with at least ten names and checkmarks on it.

"I think you're amazing," Monte said.

He sat down on the sofa next to her and kissed her forehead.

"Hey, didn't I ask you to call me from the station? I would have picked you up," Monte said, remembering his earlier instructions to her.

"Stop being ridiculous. You were busy and there's a taxi stand right outside of the station," Torie said.

She placed a hand on his forearm and rubbed gently.

"Thank you," Monte said. "Wait a minute, you're here!" Monte exclaimed, suddenly realizing that Torie was actually in his home. "That means you met the boys?"

"Yes, I did. Joshua opened the door for me, like a little gentleman. Just as I expected, they are their daddy's sons. Handsome as they want to be."

"That's just how we Lewises do!" Monte exclaimed.

"Anyway," Torie continued, swatting Monte playfully. "I introduced myself, and we talked for a few minutes about school and that little Carey Ann Washington who he's been giving the chocolate pudding Cheryl packs for him."

"Carey Ann who?"

"Ssh! Don't say anything, but looks like you aren't the only Lewis man who likes to bribe his women with food. Anyway, I also met Josiah, who's in the back practicing the latest Madden video game. I told him what my high score is so I think he's a little scared of me."

"Don't tell me you play Madden, girl."

"Yep. You didn't know that I'm a Play Station fanatic, did you? Josiah promised to give me a run for my money later." Torie laughed.

"That sounds like Josiah. He thinks he's the king of video games. Highly competitive, that one," Monte said.

"I can guess where he gets that from," Torie said. "What's that?" she asked, motioning to the box Monte held on his lap.

Monte opened the box and handed one of the flyers to Torie. They were silent as they studied his mother's face. The picture he'd given to Detective Smythe had been taken on a cruise for seniors his mother had gone on four years ago with a few of her friends. It was a beautiful close-up of her at one of the formal dinners held onboard. She was wearing a black cocktail dress and her silver hair was pulled up into a neat bun.

"She looks a lot different from this now. Mostly, in her eyes. They were so bright and clear here, but now there's this cloud in her gaze. It's like all of the confusion in her mind is played out in her eyes," Monte said.

"She's beautiful," Torie commented.

Monte was quiet. All day he had been trying to keep the worst-case scenario from entering his thought process, but it was beginning to settle in on him. It had been hours since his mother's disappearance, and it was as if she had disappeared off the face of the earth.

"Daddy, can Miss Torie come to our room?" Josiah asked as he came bounding into the living room.

"Uh, little man, maybe later—"

"Sure, Josiah, I'd love to," Torie said, patting Monte on the knee before rising. "Why don't you continue making calls," she suggested, handing the yellow pages over to Monte.

Monte watched as Josiah grabbed Torie's hand and led her out of the living room and down the hallway to his room. He picked up on the phone calls where Torie's last checkmark indicated she'd left off. Happy Time Nursery School.

When the doorbell rang hours later, Monte was just about to search for a fourth time. He and Torie had gone out, driving to surrounding towns and posting flyers in store windows, at schools and at bus and train stations. He'd spoken to Detective Smythe a couple of times; he had assured him that they'd contacted police departments throughout the county and into the next two and were still out searching. It was well past sunset and Monte could no longer keep up a brave front. He'd sat the boys down and explained to them that he was worried about their grandmother. All three of them got down on their knees and said a prayer, asking God to bring Marva home safe and sound.

Cheryl had put the boys to bed and was now making a pot of coffee in the kitchen. Torie was on the sofa in the family room, nodding off. It had been a long, trying day, and while Monte felt exhaustion in every bone whenever he tried to sit down and rest, he was unable to remain in one position for more than a few minutes.

The six o'clock local news had run the photo and a description of Marva. At the sight of her smiling on the television set Monte had had to excuse himself from the room. He stood in the bathroom, running the water and trying to force back the tears that soaked his face. It was like Shawna all over again; although the circumstances were so different, the dread and paralyzing fear were the same. He banged his hand on the side of the porcelain sink and cursed through clenched teeth. When he finally came out of the bathroom, Torie was standing in the hallway. She studied his face for a moment before moving close to him and sliding her arms around his back. She held him silently and, for a few moments, he allowed himself to be held. Monte realized that this time was different because, unlike when he lost Shawna, he had someone to help him through the pain.

Detective Smythe had said that the next course of action would be to organize search teams and bloodhounds to go out at daybreak to scour the wooded areas of town and of the neighboring areas. Monte shuddered at that statement, knowing that the expectation of the search would be to find his mother's body. After hours of uncertainty, Monte was trying to steel himself for the worse, knowing that he'd have to get the boys through the second dark cloud in their short lives.

When the bell rang, Monte rushed from the kitchen table to the front door. He yanked the door open to find his mother, wrapped in a wool blanket and flanked by two police officers.

"Mama, thank God. Mama, are you okay?" Monte asked.

He enveloped his mother in his arms and pulled her gently into the foyer. She seemed even smaller and more fragile than he remembered as he maneuvered her into the house. Both Cheryl and Torie came running at the sound of his voice.

"Glory be, thank you, Jesus," Cheryl said, lifting her arms, palms up, into the air.

"She hasn't said anything, Mr. Lewis, since we found her, but she appears to be in good physical condition," one of the officers said.

"Mama? Are you hurt?" Monte asked, looking down into his mother's round face.

"I'm fine, William. I don't need you making a big fuss over me," Marva said at last.

She'd called Monte by his father's name, immediately clueing Monte in on the fact that her mind was in another time and another place.

"My father," Monte explained to the officers who nodded understandingly.

"Mrs. Lewis, why don't I help get you into bed. I'm sure you're tired," Cheryl said, moving to Marva's side.

"Yes, child, I had a long day at work. Thank you," Marva said.

Monte stepped aside as his mother looped her arm through Cheryl's and shuffled slowly down the hallway. He turned to the police officers.

"Thank you, officers, for bringing her home," he said.

"No problem, sir. It seems she hitched a ride from someone. Probably out on Route 25, as near as we can figure. Anyway, the person probably thought he was doing a good thing. He dropped her off at the Presbyterian Missionary in Huntington. That's a homeless shelter run by the church. Apparently, she mixed in with the other residents, and it was hours before they realized that she wasn't a regular. One of the workers recalls noticing her sometime during lunch, but it wasn't until bed check that they really paid attention to her. They contacted the sheriff's office over there and, from the bulletin they'd received earlier, they immediately knew who she was."

"I can't believe this," Monte said, "I can't believe she made it that far. Well, thank you again, officers, for all your efforts today."

"We're just glad we had a good outcome. You'll probably want to take her in to see her doctor tomorrow, but like I said, she appears to be in good condition. No signs of any injuries or anything. Good night, Mr. Lewis."

Monte closed the door behind the officers and leaned heavily against it. He opened his arms to Torie, who moved in front of him, and she wrapped hers around his waist.

"I didn't believe in miracles until now, but this definitely ranks, doesn't it?" Monte asked.

"Nope, this wasn't a miracle. This one was called good old-fashioned faith and prayer," Torie said, squeezing Monte as tightly as she could.

That night, after Monte had checked in on his sleeping mother, who Cheryl had helped bathe and change into new bedclothes before securing her in bed, he made sure the guardrails were in place on her bed. After giving Cheryl the following day off and seeing her out, he double bolted the front and back doors and placed the keys on top of a bookshelf where his mother would be unable to find them. He intended to contact the alarm company in the morning and have some sort of sensor placed on the door to his mother's bedroom so that he would receive a signal if she opened the door. He and Torie settled into his bed and, with his arms wrapped securely around her, Monte's worn-out body succumbed to the most restful night of sleep he'd had in ages.

Chapter 12

Lights, Cameras...Action

Torie arrived at the first day of a two-week scheduled rehearsal period and from the moment she walked onto the set she felt as though she were finally home. Everything she had done in her life up to this point was nothing more than practice for the moment that now lay before her. She had never felt more confident and more ready.

She met her fellow cast members, some of whom she had idolized for their previous work on television and in movies. Although she'd expected to feel somewhat intimidated by working on a pilot for a show that boasted a fine cast of experienced veterans, it was, in fact, quite the opposite. Everyone was down-to-earth and extremely cordial, and after just a few days, it began to take on the feeling of a family as opposed to a group of coworkers at a job.

Torie was complimented by the other actors, as well as some of the show's producers, on her perfect memory of her lines and her ability to ad-lib when needed. Two days before taping was to begin, there were substantial script changes made and Torie and the others worked the new lines in without a hitch. Torie felt like a seasoned professional, in this, her debut.

"I can't wait until we've taped these episodes and the network sees them. I'm telling you, Monte, this is going to be a fantastic show," Torie said, excitedly using her fork to stab at a piece of lettuce in her salad.

She was seated across the table from Lisette, with Lisette's boyfriend, Jean Paul, to her left and Monte to her right. Their celebration tonight was twofold—Lisette wanted to congratulate Torie on her anticipated success with the show, and they were christening Lisette and Jean Paul's chic new Upper East Side penthouse apartment. Jean Paul, an interior designer by trade, had taken what amounted to an empty shell and designed the entire space. He'd captured the very essence of Lisette's tastes in areas like the kitchen, dining room, master bedroom and bath. The living room was a modern room, styled in earth tones, with bright walls and paintings, and there was also a large guest bedroom, an entertainment room with an at-home theater system and a balcony that had the beauty and warmth of a tropical rain forest.

"I can't wait to add you to my weekly must-see television-viewing lineup. It's going to be so cool watching my girl do her thing once a week on the tube—provided you don't come on at the same time as any of the *CSI* TV shows. Then I'll have to TiVo your behind," Lisette said.

The table broke out in raucous laughter. What was most funny to Torie was that she wholeheartedly believed Lisette's statement because, in all the years she'd known her, there was absolutely nothing that could come between her and Horatio Caine.

After dinner, the men volunteered to handle the cleanup while Lisette and Torie settled down in the entertainment room. The minute they were alone, Lisette gave Monte an enthusiastic seal of approval.

"*Mami,* that man is hot. *Ai, Papi es muy guapo.*"

"You're a sick puppy," Torie said.

"I'm serious. You know I don't usually go for those suit-type guys. You see Jean Paul. Last year I had to practically beat him into a jacket for my sister's wedding. But, *chica,* Monte is fine. He's got that whole Johnnie Cochran meets Denzel Washington thing going on. And he's not uptight like most suits. Nice open smile. He looks people dead in the eye when he's talking to them, like he's actually listening. And as if all that's not enough, he takes good care of his body and health. Nice teeth, clear skin… You done good, kid, really."

"You saw all of that over dinner?" Torie marveled.

"Girl, if there's two things I've got an eye for it's shoes and men, and not necessarily in that order. Monte Lewis is a ten if I've ever seen one."

Lisette winked and nodded her head conspiratorially. Getting the seal of approval from a best friend was a load off a woman's mind, and Torie knew that getting Lisette to endorse someone Torie was dating was truly a big deal. Lisette was what you'd call a hard sell.

"Well, that's big coming from you. You never like anyone I date," Torie stated.

"That's not true. Ooh," Lisette said, smacking Torie playfully on her thigh. "You make me sound like your mother or, even worse, my mother before she passed," she said, making the sign of the cross in front of her chest and kissing the cross she wore around her neck.

"That is so true. You hated Roberto, the cute Cuban guy I dated freshman year in college—"

"Torie, he was a full head shorter than you, and I could probably braid all of the hair he had on his back! And what was up with his sister bringing him dinner on campus every night? Talk about an L-seven."

Lisette placed her thumb and pointer finger in the shape of and *L* and pressed it against her forehead.

"Okay, what about Ike, that fine wide receiver with the tight end?" Torie giggled.

"Oh, no, you did not go there. Let's start with the fact that he was as dumb as a doorstop. You spent more time sophomore year helping him with his assignments than doing your own. I thought you were going to flunk out. And the boy had a serious case of B.O."

"Now, Lisette, that's just mean. He couldn't help sweating so much—he worked out a lot." Torie laughed.

"So what? The brother never heard of soap and water? Some body wash? Cologne? *Fabreze* odor spray? Something!" Lisette snapped. "Shoot, if he was my man, I would have rubbed one of those little pine-scented car-freshener tags all up under his armpits."

Torie collapsed against the back of the sofa, choking on her laughter. Lisette had always had that effect on her, making Torie dizzy from mirth even when she didn't want to crack a smile.

"And before you bring up that weird-looking guy from English class or the kid who's dad owned the meat market in town, just don't. They were both hot messes."

"Jeez, I can't believe you remember every guy I've dated since college. What are you doing, keeping a record of my love life?"

"Somebody has to. If left to your own devices, I don't know who you'd end up with."

"All right, Miss Know-It-All, how do you account for the fact that you absolutely loved Kevin at first?"

"Now that's an overstatement. I didn't love Kevin. I said he was gorgeous. I also distinctly remember warning you about dating basketball players. But see, you never want to learn from my mistakes. No matter how many times I trip and fall, you will go right down the same path. You've got to get out there and bump that big pumpkin of yours yourself before you believe me."

"That's not the way it is. Just because the path is the same it does not mean the journey's going to be the same."

"Save that new-age nonsense for somebody else, *chica*. Who was the one who told you that it wasn't a good idea for you to go to Spain with Kevin?"

"That would be you, O Wise One," Torie said, lowering her head and arms at the same time to feign as though she were bowing down to Lisette.

"And who was it who flew all the way to Spain, dried your tears and then went with you to kick in the door of that chick's apartment to catch that lying cheat playing naked Twister game?"

"You, O All-knowing Goddess."

"All right, then. And you still owe me for the boot I ruined on that thick-assed door," Lisette reminded.

"Oh, would you let that go already!" Torie exclaimed.

"Seriously, though, Torie, I've really got a good feeling about Monte. He seems like a genuinely decent guy. And the way he looks at you...whoo-wee! He's got it bad for you, *mi amor*."

Torie held her tongue, not wanting to let slip the fact that she, too, had it bad for him. Monte had gotten under her skin in a way that both exhilarated and frightened her. She suspected that Lisette already knew that, but Torie felt that as long as she didn't give words to her feelings, perhaps she could ignore the depth of them. Ever since the scare they'd had with his mother and the night Torie had spent with him in his home, she'd found it more and more difficult to keep her emotions in check. When Monte casually mentioned wanting to take the boys away over the winter holidays, perhaps skiing in Colorado or on a cruise or to someplace warm, he'd slipped in a comment about hoping that her acting schedule would allow her to travel with them. Torie's response had been an enthusiastic and meaningful, "I hope so, too."

It wasn't that her reservations had disappeared. Indeed, they had intensified. As a result, Torie was at war with herself, feeling her emotions deepening from attraction, to a strong like, to what they were now—love.

Monte and Jean Paul entered the entertainment room, one carrying a tray of coffee, creamer and sweeteners and the other carrying slices of the caramel cheesecake Torie had baked the night before.

"Miss Celebrity, I can't believe you baked this cheesecake yourself. It is delicious," Jean Paul said setting his tray down.

"I told you my baby can burn." Monte beamed.

"Why, thank you…both of you. Wait a minute, Jean Paul, just how do you know my cake is good already?" Torie teased.

"Because he was picking at it the entire time we were making the coffee," Monte ratted.

The group laughed as they settled in for dessert and conversation. Jean Paul put a Carlos Santana CD in the player, providing the perfect background tunes to complement the evening. They joked and talked well into the night, an easy mood guiding their dialogue. By the end of the evening, though not surprised, Torie was pleasantly comforted by how well Monte had gotten along with two of the most important people in her life. As they said their goodbyes at the door, Torie could not help but acknowledge to herself that if things didn't work with Monte, the chances that she'd ever find another man of whom Lisette approved were slim to none.

Chapter 13

Shadow of Doubt

"Darius, would you please tell your mother to lay off." Torie groaned.

"How come whenever she gets into one of her moods, she's got to be *my* mother? Shoot, she wears me down just as much as she does you." Darius laughed.

"All right now, you two, don't forget I'm still your mother. Neither one of you are too old for a strapping," Brenda said.

The trio, seated in Brenda Turner's living room in Atlanta, exchanged looks before both Torie and Darius cracked up hysterically. The stern countenance Brenda wore did not assuage their laughter and, eventually, Brenda could not help but chuckle herself. Torie was glad to see a smile on her mother's face because, since she'd arrived in Atlanta the night before, all she'd seen was Brenda's perpetual frown. Torie had flown down to spend the weekend with her mother in celebration of Brenda's birthday, yet Brenda's pessimism was quickly dampening the celebratory mood.

"Mama, you really just need to relax and trust us. Your kids are grown, you did a great job raising us and now you need to have faith that we know what we're doing in our lives," Torie said.

"She's right, Mama. Stop spending your time worrying about us and enjoy your life," Darius chimed.

"I can't help but to worry about you two because you don't always make the best decisions. I mean, now, Torie, you've landed your show finally and I couldn't be happier. I think you're going to do just great on it and your career is finally going to take off," Brenda said.

"'Finally,' she said," Torie echoed in Darius's direction.

"Finally." He smiled.

"Let me finish. I'm just trying to say that all your hard work has not gone unnoticed and I'm just happy to see that you're finally …" Brenda trailed off, catching herself. "You're getting your break at last."

"But?" Torie asked.

"But…I thought we agreed that you needed to take some time to yourself. You said you weren't going to date for at least a year and, honey, after that whole thing with Kev—"

"Mama," Torie warned.

"Well, something's got you beaming a hundred watts."

"I'm just happy about life, Mama. I'm happy to be alive… happy you're alive. We're celebrating another birthday together. What's not to smile about," Torie had replied.

Brenda kept at it until finally she hit the nail right on the head the next day.

"Now, Torie girl, I want you to tell me what on earth are you so smiley-faced about, and I mean to know right now!" she'd demanded.

Torie put on the most stern face she could muster, hoping that a show of toughness would force Brenda to back down.

"Mama, can we please not do this again?"

Brenda returned Torie's stony gaze with one of her own. Suddenly, recognition flooded her eyes.

"You've fallen in love with somebody, haven't you?" Brenda wanted to know.

"In love? No, no way. Okay, Mama, here's the thing. I've met someone and he's a really, really great man. We've been dating for a few weeks and I like him. I'm in *like,* Mama. Strong *like,* but not love, nowhere near it. We're taking things nice and slow," Torie answered.

"Oh, Torie, we agreed—"

"Mama, I know what I'm doing so please just let it be," Torie pleaded.

"Uh-uh…I'm sorry, but this needs to be said. You are still vulnerable and I'm sure this person could see that a mile away."

"Mama, Monte's not like that."

Torie felt herself growing angry and she fought to remain cool. She'd toyed with the idea of not even telling her mother about Monte, but from the moment she'd walked through the front door the evening before, her mother had been hounding her. It seemed that Brenda's powers of perception had not dulled with another year of life.

From that point on Brenda had peppered her with a million and one questions, and it was a mentally exhausted Torie who finally called the inquisition to a halt.

"Mama, enough. I didn't come down here with the intention of telling you about Monte, but now that you know, please just let me enjoy it. I don't know where this thing is headed and, frankly, I don't care right now. I just want to keep feeling what I'm feeling, keep on working and just taking pleasure from my life, however it comes."

Like an alligator with its chops around an unsuspecting mammal, Brenda pursued the conversation. In an effort to rescue Torie and her love life out of the line of fire, Darius chimed in and dropped some news of his own.

"Guess what, Mama? Sheila's pregnant again."

"What? Boy, don't play with me. How are you just going to burst out with something like that?"

"Well, we weren't planning on telling anyone until she got through the first trimester. The last miscarriage was really hard on her, but...I just couldn't hold on to the news anymore."

"Oh, my goodness. Praise God. How far along is she?" Brenda asked.

"She just hit ten weeks and everything is looking good. She's been having a little morning sickness—not much, though—and she's been very tired, but other than that—"

"Well, praise God," Brenda said. "See now, I knew something was going on when you said she wasn't coming out with us tonight. Well, that's all right."

She wrapped her arms around Darius's neck, and he threw Torie a quick smile over his mother's shoulder. Torie mouthed a solemn thank-you in return.

"You tell her I said to take it easy. Don't try to do too much. These young women nowadays think they can just rip and run while they're carrying a child. Just because women have been having babies for centuries doesn't mean that it's not hard work. You tell her I said to stay off her feet as much as possible. I'm going to cook up some dinners for you two and you come by and get them. Keep the freezer full so she don't have to worry about cooking and stuff every night, you hear?"

"Yeah, Mama. Thanks. Now you've got to promise not to say anything for another few weeks. I'll let you know when it's okay."

"All right, all right. I won't say a word," Brenda promised.

Darius looked at her doubtfully, but didn't speak on it. "Look, you two, you'd better start getting dressed if we're going to have time for dinner before the concert."

"Ooh, yes, you're right. I'm going to take my shower right now. Torie, are your clothes pressed?"

"Yes, Mama. Go on into the bathroom. Don't worry about me," Torie said. To Darius she said, "Congratulations, baby brother. Make sure you give Sheila my love."

For the remainder of her visit, Brenda was slightly preoccupied with prayers and plans for her first grandbaby, thus keeping at bay her voice of dissent about Torie's relationship with Monte. While grateful for the reprieve that Darius and Sheila's good news gave her, Torie knew that it would just be a matter of time before her mother zeroed in on her again. Yet, even the thought of having to address her mother's negativity could not burst the cloud of joy being with Monte had her riding on.

Chapter 14

Trouble in Paradise

"Torie, Torie Turner, over here."

Torie turned away from Monte in response to the voice calling her name. It was Martin Hunt, one of her costars from *Higher Learning*. He was waving at her from his position near the buffet table. He was standing with another of their costars, Lana Anderson, as well as two men whom Torie did not know.

"Do you mind, sweetheart?" she asked Monte.

"Not at all. This is your night, babe," he responded.

He picked up their drinks from the bar where they'd been standing and followed Torie across the room.

"Hey, Miss Costar. There's a couple of guys over here dying to meet you. They've been going on and on about that gorgeous Torie Turner. Now, I told them that they were exaggerating just a little bit. But I figured I'd introduce them to you, anyway," Martin joked.

Torie made a fist and drove it slowly into Martin's bicep.

"Beautiful and a bruiser...my kind of woman," the taller, olive-complexioned man said.

"Torie Turner, Alex Dibiasi and Boris Carson. These

gentlemen are the directors of the award-winning independent film, *Canary Blown*," Martin said.

"Yes, gentlemen, nice to meet you. Excellent film. I cried like a baby," Torie said, shaking each man's hand in turn. "I'd like you all to meet Monte Lewis, attorney-at-law. Monte, Alex, Boris, Martin and Lana."

"Hey, man. Ouch, Tor, you travel with your attorney at your side? Talk about being a shrewd negotiator," Martin joked.

Monte did not miss the look in Martin's eyes as he spoke. He knew the signs of being sized up by another man. He also did not miss the look in Martin's eyes when he looked at Torie, or the familiar tone of voice he used when speaking to her. Monte was not an insecure man, nor was he a man who felt the need to measure himself against other men. He was confident in who he was and, more importantly, he was confident in his relationship with Torie. However, like a warrior lion in the age-old game of mating, he knew that sometimes he might be forced to mark his territory. That way, there would be no confusion on anyone's part. He moved closer to Torie.

"Here, babe," Monte said, handing Torie a glass of Grand Marnier cognac.

He looked meaningfully at Martin while taking a long sip from his own glass.

"Thank you. Martin, behave yourself tonight," Torie said. "Gentlemen, it was a pleasure meeting you. I'd like to introduce Monte to a few more people. Excuse us."

As the pair walked away, Monte placed one hand at the small of Torie's back. He did not bother to look behind him because his point had been made, loud and clear.

The party was one of those affairs to which, as an entertainment lawyer, Monte had had his share of invitations but, over his career, he had often avoided attending. It was an industry gathering, full of television, movie and music folks. He knew many of the people gathered there and could count on one hand the individuals with whom he'd have the stomach to share more than a passing pleasantry. He had never been attracted to the so-called beautiful people of the world and, despite the fact that he had chosen entertainment law as a career path, he was not interested in becoming what he liked to call celebrity seekers—people who hung on, attending every industry event, wanting to be seen and rub elbows with the rich, famous and glamorous. He'd come to this party solely because Torie had invited him to be her escort for the evening. He'd have had breakfast with the devil if Torie had invited him, so surely, he reasoned, he can make it through one little party.

At one point in the evening, Monte felt an overwhelming urge to hold Torie in his arms. He whispered in her ear, took her hand and led her to the dance floor. An old Smokey Robinson tune was playing. He folded Torie in his arms and she leaned against him. They moved together as if they had been dance partners for years, having already grown accustomed to the feel and rhythm of each other.

"If I asked you to slip out of here with me right now, take me back to your place and take advantage of me, what would you say?" Monte said, staring into Torie's eyes.

"I would say that while nothing would give me more pleasure, you know that I can't leave just yet."

Monte pouted.

"Oh, stop that. You look just like Josiah."

"Speaking of whom, the boys want to know when you're coming over again. Joshua's been rehearsing for a school play he's in and he wants you to read lines with him. He says I keep missing my cues. And I think Josiah's got a crush on you." Monte laughed.

"Aww, Monte, I don't know when I'm going to get some free time. With rehearsals and tapings six days a week, running until very late in the evening sometimes, and then me needing to be at the studio early every day, it's a little hectic right now."

"So what? You can come out in the evening, sleep over and I can drive you back in the morning," Monte said. "Or you can come out when you wrap at the studio on Saturday night. You're off on Sundays. That way, we can spend the whole day together."

Torie did not respond right away. She chewed the inside of her bottom lip, feeling once again the conflict within her brewing. No matter how many times she told herself to slow things down, she found her heart moving full speed ahead. Yet it was getting increasingly more difficult to navigate in this sea of emotions, and she knew that it was no longer just a matter of hers and Monte's feelings. Now his sons were involved and, while an adult could be expected to understand emotional hang-ups and reservations, children could not. The last thing she wanted to do was hurt Monte's children.

"Let's figure this out later," Torie said.

She avoided looking Monte in the eye and, from that and the tone of her voice, Monte knew that something was amiss. He let the subject die for the time being, but he knew that it was something they would need to get to the bottom of sooner rather than later. They continued to dance for the next two songs in silence, each of them feeling a sudden invisible barrier forming between them. Finally, Torie excused herself to use the restroom and Monte headed to the bar for a refill. While he stood there, waiting for the bartender to prepare his drink, he was so lost in his own thoughts that he didn't notice Martin's approach until the man was standing at his side.

"So, Monte, was it? Having a good time?" he asked.

"Hey, Martin. Yes, thanks for asking," Monte said, turning to face the man.

"Don't tell me Torie abandoned you? She's always on the move. I tell you, you should see her on set. The rest of us have to drink at least two cans of Red Bull energy drink in order to keep up with her," Martin said.

"Really? That's interesting," Monte replied.

He was really not in the mood for the little game Martin was trying to play with him. He was irritated by his unfinished conversation with Torie, distracted, and the last thing he wanted to do was spar with this two-bit, Sidney Poitier wannabe.

"Yeah, she's something else. I really admire how hard she works. But I keep telling her that all work and no play…well, you know what I mean."

"You're right about that. That's why we make sure to carve out time to relax and enjoy ourselves. It keeps us young and healthy," Monte said.

"That's good. A few of us on the show were talking about getting some downtime the other day. Someone suggested we take a little trip, you know, to someplace warm for a few days. Cast only—no significant others, no distractions. It'll give us a chance to critique ourselves and our performances while we unwind. Torie said she thought it was a good idea. Did she mention it to you?" Martin asked.

Monte clenched his lower and upper teeth together, the muscle in his jaw flinching ever so slightly. He chided himself at the exact same moment for allowing Martin to get to him in this way.

"I think that's a really good idea. My colleagues at the firm take retreats together several times a year. You've got to form a strong relationship with your coworkers in order to have a solid working environment. Also, it's good for some of the less stellar performers to spend time with the pros—gives them a chance to get some tips to help improve their game a little. Good luck with that," Monte said.

He picked up his drink from the bar and slipped a five-dollar bill in the bartender's tip jar.

"If you'll excuse me," Monte said.

He didn't wait for Martin's response before heading toward Torie, who had just reentered the room. They remained at the party for another hour, during which Monte chatted with a couple of other lawyers who were present while Torie talked more with the show's producers and others. He noticed Martin hanging around her like a little puppy waiting for scraps to fall from the dinner table, but he didn't have the energy or the desire to play guard dog. He kept his distance and trusted in the fact that Martin's flirting would have no effect on Torie, because at the end of the night it was Monte who she'd leave with.

Chapter 15

Too Good to Be True

Torie paced nervously in the reception area of the news station where Lisette worked. She'd been informed by the receptionist that Lisette was still wrapping up a segment and would be available to see her shortly. She thought she'd wear a hole in the carpet before those doors leading to the inner offices opened, but what seemed liked hours was actually only a few long minutes.

"Ms. Turner, you're free to go in now," the receptionist said at long last.

Torie made a beeline for the glass doors when the receptionist pressed the button that released their lock. She walked down the gray-carpeted hallway, passing by frosted-glass-partitioned offices of various other producers and studio personnel. Lisette was standing in front of her office door when Torie approached.

"What on earth is going on? You had poor Diane out at reception nervous as I don't know what. She left me two e-mails and three voice-mail messages that you were out there waiting for me," Lisette said.

"I'm sorry, I just had to see you," Torie said.

She bustled past Lisette and stalked into her office. She plopped down on the nearest chair, threw her purse on top of Lisette's cluttered desk and covered her face in her hands.

"Okay, now you're really scaring me," Lisette said.

She closed the door and pulled another chair directly in front of the one Torie was seated in. She grabbed both of Torie's wrists and pulled her hands roughly from her face.

"What's going on?"

"We just got word that the show's been picked up by NBC for a full season," Torie said.

"What? That's great. Oh, man, that is fabulous. You are on your way, girl. You should be bouncing off of the walls."

"No, no, no…you don't understand. It's not as simple as that. The show has been picked up but it's going to be taped on the west coast…probably Los Angeles."

It took Lisette a moment to absorb Torie's statement. She paused, still holding both of Torie's wrists in her hands.

"You're moving?" she asked.

"If I want to be in this show I am," Torie said.

Suddenly the weight of Torie's dilemma and an understanding of her less-than-ecstatic mood made complete sense to Lisette.

"Oh, sweetie, I'm sorry. I mean, I'm happy for you…it's your big break, what you've been working for all this time. But I know you don't want to move again."

"I can't believe this, Lisette. It's like every time I try to convince myself that I don't have some dark cloud hanging over my head, purposely wreaking havoc in my life, there it is again, dumping buckets of hail, sleet and snow on top of me."

"No, Torie, don't say that. There's no conspiracy against you. It's just sometimes things don't work out the way we hope they will. Sometimes we just have to roll with the punches. Okay, so let's look at the positives here," Lisette said, reaching over to her desk for a writing pad and a pen. "You've got a great opportunity on a major network to showcase your talents. This will open so many doors for you that you'll have to beat casting directors down with a stick soon."

She scratched the words *great show, great network* and *opportunities* on the pad.

"The show will tape for, what, six or seven weeks at a time?"

"Twelve," Torie responded.

"Okay, twelve weeks. Then tack on a few weeks for rehearsals and publicity stuff. That'll put you in L.A. for about five months at a time. Okay, and I'm sure you could squeeze in a couple of long weekends."

Torie eyed her doubtfully.

"Or maybe not. But you could get back to New York for at least five or six months out of the year."

Lisette said this last part with a feigned lightness, knowing full well that they sounded about as gloomy as they looked on paper.

"Or I'll get more work—because, after all, that is the goal—and then by the time I see New York again—"

"Come on, Torie, don't think like that," Lisette said, rubbing her friend's shoulder.

"What am I going to do, Lisette?" Torie asked.

"What can you do? You know as well as I do that second chances are about as guaranteed as snow in July, much less third chances. Now look, I like Monte…a lot. You know that I'm pulling for you guys. But, Torie, I'm not going to sit back and watch you put another man over your career. Not again. No way, no how."

Lisette leaned back in her chair, tossing the writing pad back onto the desk. She looked her friend in the eyes defiantly, waiting for her response.

"Why does this keep happening to me?" Torie whispered at last, her head hanging low.

"Don't get all fatalistic on me, *chica*. Come on, stop looking at this as a bad thing. Maybe it's a good thing. Maybe the separation will give you some time to sort out your feelings for Monte. Figure out whether you love him enough to make a commitment."

Torie snapped her head up and made eye contact with Lisette.

"What do you mean? Who said anything about a commitment?"

"Torie, please don't make me slap you. Do you think I'm stupid? You're in love with that man, and you know it. You're just too damned afraid, or proud or both, to admit it, but if you want to live in denial that's fine. Just don't try to pull me into your bed of abjuration, because I'm not a believer."

"I don't know what I feel, Lisette," Torie conceded. "I just don't know how to be dedicated to my career and give my all to someone at the same time. I feel like I'm trying to cut my heart into two pieces and sharing them with both my loves. Monte is such a good man and he doesn't deserve this. Sometimes I think it might be best if I get out of his life and leave room for him to find love with someone who can be dedicated to him and those boys."

Torie stood abruptly and, running her hand through her hair, walked toward the picture window at the far end of Lisette's office. She looked out at the darkening sky, the city skyline before her eyes.

"Why don't you think you are that person?" Lisette wanted to know.

"Because right now I'm about to choose my career over them. I'm about to go three thousand miles away from them for the better part of the year, and I don't know that I'm going to look back," Torie said definitively.

Lisette walked to join her friend at the window. She put her arm around Torie's waist and they stood watching the sun set over Manhattan. Torie rested her head against Lisette's shoulder. They remained that way for some time, Lisette giving Torie the time she needed to soak in the enormity of her predicament. Knowing that there was only one choice that she could make and being resolute in that choice were two entirely different things.

"When are you going to see Monte?"

"I don't know. I'm not really ready to tell him about this."

"Well, it's just a matter of time before you have to and I bet he's going to be very supportive. You'll see," Lisette said.

Torie didn't tell Lisette that that was precisely what she was afraid of. Monte was an optimistic person all around, refusing to even consider the complications that would face them. Torie, on the other hand, was a realist and, realistically speaking, she was beginning to think that a long-term relationship with Monte, or anyone else for that matter, just wasn't in the near future for her. This was her big shot, perhaps a once-in-a-lifetime opportunity. Most people lied about not being interested in celebrity. They pretended that living the lifestyle of the rich and famous was not something that appealed to them. Torie would not deny to herself or anyone else that being wealthy enough to indulge her whims and notorious enough to have paparazzi sifting through her trash cans was not an exciting prospect to her. She wanted to attend the parties, do the interviews, sign the autographs and live the life of a sought-after actress. Becoming a wife and mother to two boys overnight paled in comparison to all that. Yet, she also knew that leaving Monte and the boys behind would hurt her more than a little bit.

Chapter 16

Confessions

Monte waited until the boys were tucked into their beds and sound asleep before he broached the subject that had been dominating his mind for the past few weeks. Every time he tried to raise the topic, Torie evaded it, making it obvious to Monte that they had a problem brewing that was a lot bigger than he'd first believed it to be. Torie had come out to the lake house with him and the boys early on a Monday morning and they'd spent the day fishing, canoeing on the lake and cooking the fish they'd caught. They'd played board games and video games well into the evening, before heading back home.

Marva was in stable condition. She'd begun to have fewer clear days again, but on days where she was confused or disoriented either he, Cheryl or the boys would just sit with her and talk to her or read aloud and she would remain calm. Monte felt good about taking the day with the boys and Torie. It was a crisp early autumn day and it would probably be the last of its kind before much cooler weather set in.

Monte was a little surprised when Torie accepted his invitation to join them at the lake without hesitation. It had been a week since she'd wrapped up taping for the television show, yet she remained busy reading scripts and meeting with producers. After a great day together, where he had the opportunity to watch her interact with the boys, Monte was more certain than ever that Torie was the kind of woman he could build a lasting relationship with. Tonight, however, he aimed to put his cards on the table in the hopes that she would lay all of hers out, as well. No more skirting around issues.

He prepared two cups of decaffeinated coffee and brought them to the living room where Torie was sitting on the sofa. She was wearing one of his sweatshirts, the house having developed a little chill to it, and her feet were tucked beneath her behind. Monte put the coffee mugs down and crossed the room to turn the thermostat up a few degrees. He then joined Torie on the sofa. She stretched her legs out across his lap and he took one of her slim size-seven feet in his hands and began massaging it.

"Did you have a good time today?" he asked.

"I certainly did. I didn't know you were that nice on an open grill, Mr. Lewis. Kudos to the chef," she said.

"I've got quite a few tricks up my sleeve, I'll have you know. Or should I say under my apron?" Monte retorted.

"You don't say?"

Monte exchanged one of Torie's feet for the other. He continued his massage while formulating his words.

"Torie, the past few months have been amazing. I really didn't expect this...to find someone—" Monte broke off, feeling a sudden lump in his throat where there had not been one moments before.

He cleared his throat and began again.

"I've never really talked to you about Shawna, about my life with her—"

"Monte, you don't have to. I know how much you loved her and how much you and the boys suffered after she was gone," Torie interrupted.

"No, but just hear me out. When I married Shawna, I really and truly believed that when we exchanged those vows, they meant forever. I expected us to grow old together, dance at our children's weddings, bounce grandchildren on our knees—the whole nine yards. I never anticipated that our time together would be so short."

"Most people never do," Torie said softly.

"When she got sick, it just…it just all happened so fast. In those last days, I remember praying for just one more day, one more month…one more year, with her. But finally I had to let her go. I realized that the cancer was eating her up inside and she was in agony. She tried so hard to be strong for me and the boys. She tried not to take the pain medications because they'd make her sleep and she wanted to spend as much time awake and alert for us. But the pain was just too much. It was so hard watching her suffer. At the end, I started begging God to take her so she could be at peace."

"It takes a lot of love to do that, Monte—to be so unselfish."

Monte nodded slowly, trying to make sense of what was going through his mind back then and now.

"I never thought that I would feel an ounce of what I felt for Shawna for someone else. I never even entertained that thought. Perhaps part of the reason was guilt. I thought by letting someone else in, I would betray her…us, what we had. But I've got to tell you something. From the moment I met you, from those hours we spent in that elevator, I began to think and see things differently. The time Shawna and I had together was not perfect by any means. It was full of its ups and downs, twists and turns, just the way love and marriage are supposed to be. But for whatever reason, our forever wasn't in God's plan."

Monte took a deep breath. He turned to face Torie. Looking

directly into her eyes, he felt his own growing moist in response to the deep emotions churning inside of him.

"I finally see that the love I have for Shawna will forever be a part of me. It's part of what makes me the man I am and the father my boys need. And the day I woke up and realized that I'd fallen in love with you was both the happiest and saddest day I've had in a long while, Torie."

"Monte—"

"I love you, Torie. I love you in my heart and in my soul. Believe me, I truly didn't see it coming until it hit me, and now I can't imagine not having these feelings for you, even though they make me feel somewhat conflicted," Monte said.

He picked up both of Torie's hands and held them in his. He leaned down and kissed her fingers gingerly and looked into her eyes.

"Monte," she began again, "this is so hard for me to say to you right now."

"It doesn't have to be."

"Monte, I've tried to tell myself that it is too soon for me to feel the way I do about you. I've tried to convince myself that we're just caught up in the rapture of the moment and that, when things cool down between us, we'll realize that a strong like is not the same thing as love. But dammit, Monte, if I don't love you, too. I'm in love with you and that feeling inside makes me want to sing and cry at the same time," Torie said.

"Is loving me that hard for you?" Monte asked.

He sounded hurt and Torie would have given anything to spare his feelings. Yet, she knew that to be anything less than truthful to him at this moment would be unfair.

"Loving you is like a breath of fresh air, Monte. I've never met a man with more honor and valor. I trust you. I have never been able to say that about another man—not even my own father."

"You *can* trust me, Torie, with your heart and with your life," Monte declared. "I'd never abandon you like he did."

"I know, I know. Thankfully, I never let my father's failures shape my relationships, but, Monte, I've got to tell you that I have been disappointed in love before. If I knew half of what I know now five years ago...well, let's just say that things would be different."

"Some guys are immature jerks who don't know the first thing about loving a woman. I know I'm selling my brothers out by saying this, but it's true. You can trust me, though, Torie. I know how to love you, baby. And I'm not asking you to share my love...I'm just asking you to respect what I still feel for Shawna, the mother of my children."

"I know that, and if it were just a matter of trusting you and loving you, I would be the happiest woman alive."

"But it is as simple as that. As long as we are open and honest with each other, there's nothing we can't conquer," Monte said.

"No, Monte. That's something out of a fairy tale. But, baby, this is real life and in real life, there are obstacles and challenges that can come out of left field and knock you on your butt."

"I don't care about that. Don't you think I know how hard life can be sometimes? That's all the more reason, when you find someone who fills your heart, to keep them close to your side," Monte snapped.

He felt like Torie was trying to talk him out of feeling the way he felt for her and he was growing steadily more agitated by this.

"Monte—"

"No, hold on a minute now. I'm not sure what it is you're getting at, Torie, but I really wish you'd just spit it out. I love you and you love me. Yes, there'll be problems, conflicts... things to be worked out. But, baby, being with you for these past few months has made me realize that I'd rather have someone by my side through those conflicts than to go them alone."

The first tear that sprung from Torie's eye startled Monte. He stared at her, speechless. That solitary tear was soon followed by another and another. His heart lurched. Seeing her in such emotional agony threatened to rip him in two.

"Monte, I'm not sure I can do this," Torie sobbed. "This is all too much...too fast."

"We can slow it down," Monte said.

"I don't know if I want to. Monte, there are some things about my past that I haven't shared with you. Things that I'm not very proud of. I've been working really hard to try to...I don't know, just trying to put myself first and stop tying my own personal happiness to my mate."

"And you think that I would somehow interfere with that?"

"I don't know." Torie sniffed, trying to regain control of her composure. "A while back, I made some bad choices because I thought that the man I loved loved me back. I gave up great opportunities for him. More importantly, I gave up myself. I stopped considering what made me happy, what I needed for me. I won't ever do that again," Torie finished defiantly.

"I would never ask you to do that. I don't think I would even want to be with a woman who doesn't take care of her needs first."

"Don't you see what I'm telling you, Monte? It's not about what you'd ask me to do. It's not about your feelings for your wife—I respect that, I really do. It's about me...and what I would do. It's not you that I don't trust...it's me."

At that Torie jumped up from the sofa. Sobs racked her body as she moved away from Monte. It was the first time she'd ever been this brutally honest with herself or with anyone else. It was the first time that she acknowledged that the reason why she'd vowed to concentrate on her career and avoid relationships was because she knew her track record. She did not trust herself to remain true to herself.

Monte rose and moved swiftly to where Torie stood in front of the mantel. From behind he grabbed her shoulders and pulled her until her back rested against his chest.

"I won't lose myself again, Monte. And with you…I can see that happening. Jesus, look at this," she said, sweeping her hand in front of the mantel. "Look at these pictures. You and these beautiful boys. They've been through so much already. Monte, I don't want to disappoint you and them," Torie said.

Finally, Monte understood why she'd been so hesitant about meeting the boys and spending time with them. She was afraid to get close to them and to let them get close to her, in case things did not work out or, alternatively, in case they worked out too well. She was afraid of becoming trapped.

"You won't, baby. You couldn't. We love you for who you are and I'm not asking you to be anybody else. Please, Torie, let's just try. There's no harm in trying," Monte whispered in her ear.

"People get hurt when you try and fail, Monte."

"Ssh, don't say that. Don't even think it. I love you, Torie. I'm going to tell you that every day, three times a day, until you believe that my love will hold you up and help you be strong. Until you believe that this love will only help you soar and will never hold you down. I promise, Torie."

Monte held Torie, kissing her tears until they went away. If she had underestimated how formidable a man he was, she was about to find out. Monte had no intention of letting her out of his life.

Chapter 17

Secrets

Monte woke up and glanced at the alarm clock. The red digital numbers confirmed what he already suspected due to the fact that not a sliver of sunlight peeked into his bedroom. It was just after four o'clock in the morning. He hadn't had a complete and restful night of sleep in the past five days. His rest had been uneasy and he'd had fitful dreams that kept him tossing and turning. When he awoke, he was never able to grasp a thread of what the dream had been about. All he was left with was a feeling of unease. Monte considered taking a sleep aid but was reluctant to do so. With the boys and his mother in the house, it was important to him to be able to wake up at a moment's notice in case one of them needed him.

He sat up, kicking the covers back, and swung his legs over the side of the bed. Scratching his head, Monte sighed. While he could put his finger on one issue that was causing him a lot of distress, he did not think it was the sole cause of his inability to sleep peacefully. He hated to even let the thought of his mother being a problem enter his mind, but he also could not hide from the truth of the matter. The reality was, Marva's health was on the decline. Physically, she was beginning to have more difficulty moving around and controlling her muscles. The tremors were beginning to affect the muscles controlling her swallowing and digestion. Mentally, things were about as bad as they could be. Ever since the day of her disappearance, the dementia had come back with a vengeance. Her memory was spotty and some days she found it difficult to find the words she was looking for to communicate. Monte hated to see her staring into space, but even more than that, it stabbed him in the heart every time she looked at him with a blank expression, as if she had never met him a day in her life.

He had been so hopeful just a few months back. He'd let himself believe that the medicines the doctor had prescribed were going to, if not cure her, at least help her to live a longer and happier life. Marva was only sixty-five years old and Monte could not comprehend the possibility that her life was coming to a rapid conclusion. He shuddered just to think about it, but think about it he must. He had some decisions to make and he knew that he was all alone in that. As great a help as Cheryl had been to him and his family over the years, Monte knew that she had done all that she was capable of doing. With the assistance of Marva's doctor he'd hired a morning and an evening nurse. Cheryl still came to the house in the late mornings and was there when the boys were brought home by the school bus. When Monte arrived home in the evenings, Cheryl had dinner prepared, the boys' homework was complete and laid out for Monte's review and the house was clean. The nurses were able to exercise Marva to stop her muscles from becoming completely stiff and immovable, administer her medications, bathe her and stimulate her mental faculties. After putting the boys to bed, Monte would sit with Marva, talking to her or reading to her until she fell asleep.

There were many nights that he would sit watching as his mother slept, wishing that things could be different.

Sometimes he wished that he had a sibling with whom he could share the load of her care. On the rare nights that he stayed late at the office, had a function to attend or spent the evening with Torie, Cheryl graciously agreed to stay over, either until he came home or all night. And while that helped to take a load off his mind if even for just a few hours, it was still a difficult cross to bear.

One bright spot was the fact that Torie seemed to be working through her doubts and fears. She'd spent the past two weekends with them and just having her there was a comfort. The boys began to look forward to Fridays when she would arrive and on Monday mornings they were sad to see her leave with Monte, headed back to the city. For Monte, every day brought him closer to being able to tuck the part of his heart that belonged to Shawna a little deeper inside of him. He still thought about her often—little things, like a certain food or a color triggering remembrances of the first woman he'd ever loved. However, each day also brought him closer to Torie, a woman who was very different from Shawna, and one who had pulled him slowly from the darkness of grief into the light of a second chance at happiness. Monte couldn't help worrying that, despite how good things were going, somehow he was being greedy to think that he could have magic in his life twice. What he did, instead, was cross his fingers and hope lady luck was on his side.

"Hey, Monica, how are you?" Monte asked as he entered the elevator.

"I'm well, Monte. I never see you anymore. How've you been?"

"Pretty good. I heard you're working with Ed on that New Line merger. That's a big deal. Congratulations," Monte said.

Ed Cushfield, one-half of the founding partners of the firm, always selected one of the junior associates to bring in on one of his big clients. While the young attorney believed it to be a reward for the good work he or she had been doing, which it was in some respects, others knew that it was Cushfield's way of ascertaining firsthand whether the newbie had what it took to move up the ranks. Monte fondly remembered his own such test shortly after he'd joined the firm.

"Thanks. I'm learning a lot shadowing the big guy around," Monica said. "So, I bet you'll be using up your frequent-flier miles traveling to the west coast this winter, huh?"

"No...I don't have any trips out west planned," a puzzled Monte said.

"Oh, I'm sorry...I just assumed you would be visiting Torie out there. I'm sorry I misspoke," Monica said flustered.

"Torie? Why would I have to go out west to visit Torie?"

"I shouldn't have opened my big mouth. Forget I said anything, Monte," Monica said. "I...I'm sorry."

The elevator doors opened on their floor and Monica practically ran out into the offices. Monte stepped off of the elevator slowly, his mind struggling to make sense of what Monica had said to him. Monte's first impulse was to pick up the phone and call Torie right away. He'd tell her what Monica had said to him and demand an explanation. And she would have one—one that made sense and would serve to squash the anxiety that was slowly building up in his stomach.

Before Monte could reach his office and his telephone, he was stopped by a colleague armed with an urgent development in a deal he and Monte had put together. Monte's day jumped off to a quick and eventful start. By the time he felt able to secure a few minutes of downtime to call Torie, he realized that it was already close to when he was supposed to pick her up at her apartment for dinner and the newest, hottest show to hit Broadway in years. He decided that, after waiting as long as he'd been forced to, he could wait a little longer and talk to her face-to-face.

It began raining heavily as Monte drove uptown to Torie's apartment. In the slowed traffic, Monte had plenty of time to think. The more he thought, the more his optimism about his pending conversation with Torie began to wane. Soon, his mood matched the gloomy weather and he began to contemplate not saying anything to her at all about what he'd been told. Indeed, when he arrived at Torie's apartment and she opened the door to him, all he wanted to do was pull her into his arms and kiss her until his doubts faded. He couldn't stand the thought of losing love again, but he also couldn't stand the thought that she would deliberately deceive him.

"Hey, babe," she greeted him, kissing him softly on the lips. "I'm almost ready."

Torie stepped aside and allowed Monte room to enter. Shutting the door behind him she moved in stocking feet toward her bedroom.

"Sit down for a minute. Do you want a drink?" she called over her shoulder.

"No, thanks. I'm good," Monte replied.

He crossed the entryway and stepped into the living room area. He plopped onto the sofa, sagging as though he'd been carrying a heavy load. The radio was tuned in to an AM news station, and Monte listened to the disc jockey cracking jokes about the current gas crisis. Some of it was actually funny, but Monte couldn't muster the desire to laugh. This told him that there was no way he'd be able to muster the strength to pretend that he didn't know what he knew. He had to talk to her.

Monte followed the sound of Torie's humming toward the back of her apartment. He stood in the doorway of the bedroom, watching her apply cream to her arms and neck. He still could not get over how beautiful she was. It didn't matter whether it was day or night, whether she was clothed or naked, made-up or barefaced—she was a vision of loveliness that he never tired of beholding. His gaze wandered to her bed, and he thought of the nights he'd spent in it, pleasuring her on those satin sheets. The ceiling fan that hung above the bed often spun slowly, cooling their sizzling bodies all night long. Thinking of those splendid moments made Monte want to take her where she stood.

"I know, I know. I'm hurrying. You wouldn't believe the day I had. The meeting down at the studio took three hours instead of one, I was late for my doctor's appointment so I had to sit and wait for almost an hour and then my hair stylist used some new product on my hair and had it feeling as dry as sandpaper. By the time she washed it out and did it all over again, I knew there was no way I'd make the dry cleaner to pick up the dress I wanted to wear tonight. And to top it all off, I got home to find that there's some sort of leaky pipe that's running straight down the lines at this end of the building. The landlord had a plumber in my apartment for an hour trying to figure out where the leak is coming from." Torie sighed, fussing with a few strands of hair along her temple. "But I'm ready. What time are our reservations?"

Monte didn't answer. His mouth had grown parched, and he felt as though he couldn't get enough air in his lungs.

"Monte?"

Torie turned around when he didn't answer. She looked expectantly at him.

"What's wrong?"

"Torie, we need to talk," Monte said.

"Uh-oh, sounds serious," Torie said lightly.

"It is."

Torie nodded slowly. She moved toward the bed and took a seat at the edge, keeping her eyes locked with Monte's. She patted the side of the bed next to her. Monte moved to the bed and sat down heavily beside her. He didn't look at her.

"Is there something that you aren't telling me, Torie?" he asked plainly.

"What? What do you mean?"

"It's a simple question. Is there something going on in your life that you are not telling me about?" Monte repeated.

"Monte, I'm sure I don't know what you're talking about," Torie replied.

"Let me rephrase. Is there something going on on the west coast that you're not telling me about?"

Torie's heart skipped a beat. She didn't answer right away, but merely dropped her head slightly, her eyes cast on the floor. The seconds ticked by almost audibly as neither of them dared to move or speak, for fear of what the next words from the other would be.

"Who told you?" Torie questioned at last.

"Who told me?" Monte looked at her incredulously. "Is that the first thing that comes to mind—who told me? Who told me what, Torie? That my woman has been keeping a secret from me? That the person I've laid my heart out on the line for, the woman I've been sharing my bed and my life with, is not being honest with me?"

"Monte, please let me explain."

"Oh, yes, please do. Explain this to me, Torie, nice and slowly, because right now it's not making one bit of sense."

"Monte, I wanted to tell you. I tried…I just couldn't find the words. Shortly after we found out the show was being picked up, we were told that, because the taxes charged by the city of New York for series productions is so high, the network went looking for alternative locations. I didn't really think much of it at the time because the series is based on New Yorkers and life in the Big Apple. When we got the final word…I couldn't believe it. They decided to move the show to Los Angeles for at least the first two seasons."

"When, Torie? When did you find this out?"

"A few weeks ago," Torie admitted. "I really wanted to tell you, Monte. I just didn't know how. I didn't know how you would take the news."

Monte stood and walked a few paces away from Torie. He didn't turn to face her, just couldn't at that moment. His face was crestfallen, and he didn't trust his voice.

"Monte, baby, please talk to me. Tell me what you're thinking," Torie pleaded.

Monte shook his head slowly from side to side. Disbelief was the reigning emotion in him at that moment. He could not make himself believe that this was happening. Just when he thought that he was finally headed for happier times, life had sent him yet another curveball. But he was tired of the game. Tired of trying to keep his head up and seeing nothing but clouds on the horizon.

He finally turned to face Torie. She rose and came to stand in front of him. He wanted to reach out and pull her to him, to convince himself and her at the same time that it would be okay. Yet, for the first time in their relationship he didn't believe that.

"Why couldn't you just tell me?" he asked.

"I don't know," she said.

"So were you planning to just pack up and send me a postcard?"

"No, Monte. Of course not. I would have told you... somehow, soon. I know I would have."

"I'm not so sure, Torie. I'm not sure of anything right now." Monte pressed his forefingers to his eyes. "I need some air," he said.

He took two steps backward, moving toward the bedroom door.

"Monte, wait. Please, let's just talk about this."

"I...I need to go," he said.

He kept moving until he was at the apartment door. He turned the knob and paused. He heard Torie call his name, but he couldn't go back. He needed time to think, to clear his head. Monte walked out, shutting the door behind him. The next thing he knew he was in his car, driving through the rain. He drove blindly, without thinking about where he was going. Eventually, he pulled into his own driveway in Sands Point; he turned off the car and sat in the darkness. He felt his phone vibrating in his pocket again. This time, he didn't bother to look at the display. Torie had called three times since he'd left her, but he wasn't ready to talk. He could not think of anything they had to say to each other.

Chapter 18

Pride Is a Poor Substitute

The ball whizzed past Monte's racket, in no danger of being struck.

"Point game," Kurt Dunlevy called.

"Monte, you're killing us. Come on, we can still win this. Get your head in the game," Brent said, patting Monte on the back.

Monte nodded. He got into position, bent his legs at the knee and focused on the serve. It took Kurt and his partner, Jeffrey, a full two additional minutes to put the game away. They shook hands and offered a rematch, which Monte declined.

"All right, what's up, man?" Brent asked as they headed back to the locker room.

"I'm just a little tired, man. Haven't been sleeping well lately," Monte said, trying to shrug the loss of the game as no big deal.

Brent wasn't fooled. He considered his friend for a minute before speaking.

"Does that lame response mean you don't want to talk

about it or that it's too painful to talk about just yet?" Brent said as he popped the combination lock on his locker.

Monte chuckled, which was the closest he'd come to a smile in days.

"I guess a little bit of both," he said.

"All right, man, I won't pry. But I will tell you this. Sometimes things seem worse than they really are when you keep them locked inside your head. Talk about it and, voilà, a molehill instead of a mountain."

"I hear you, man. Thanks," Monte said.

The truth was that Monte didn't trust himself not to break down at the mere mention of Torie's name. He hadn't spoken to her since he'd walked out of her apartment three days ago. He felt like a heel in the way he was handling the news that she was relocating to the west coast, a childish one at that. Monte was more upset with himself than with Torie. He had heard the warning bells, had seen the hesitance from her, but he had pushed ahead, anyway. He'd let his heart lead his mind and logic because unconsciously he had been starved for the love and companionship of a woman. Torie had hit that soft spot inside of him that he thought had long ago turned to stone. With her beauty, grace, talent, intelligence and humor, she'd dusted the frost off his soul and made him believe in second chances. The truth was that Monte was terrified that his second chance had just slipped through his fingers. Maybe he'd been wrong, after all, to even try for a second chance at love.

Their lunchtime exercise over, Monte and Brent returned to the office. Monte had just sat down behind his desk, determined to plow through the pile of documents in front of him before quitting time at five o'clock, when his secretary buzzed him.

"Mr. Lewis, Ms. Turner is headed back to see you. Is that all right?" Margaret said.

It was no secret around the office that Monte and Torie were seeing each other—at least, it was definitely not a secret from Margaret. Margaret had been Monte's right-hand woman since he'd become a senior associate, six years ago. She was a woman of a certain age, who understood the value of discretion in both professional and personal matters. Monte trusted Margaret with the most sensitive information and she had never once betrayed him.

"Uh, Margaret, can you, uh, tell her…just tell her I'm busy?" Monte stammered into the handset.

"Well, then, I'll wait," Torie said.

She was standing in the doorway, one hand resting on the knob. The look on her face told Monte that he could not run anymore.

"Never mind, Margaret," he said, pressing the release button on the telephone.

He slowly returned the handset to its cradle and stood from his desk. Torie moved farther into the office and closed the door behind her. There was a deafening silence for the first few moments. Monte moved to one of the low-back chairs in front of his desk. Torie took the seat next to him. She laid her purse in her lap, adjusted and readjusted it. No longer able to withstand the agony of the lack of sound, Monte spoke.

"I should have called you," he said.

"Yes, you should have," Torie replied.

"I was upset. But that was no reason to ignore your calls. I'm sorry," Monte said.

"And I'm sorry…for keeping you in the dark, for not being honest with you."

Torie sighed. She'd been waiting three days to say those words, and now that they were out, she felt as if a brick had been lifted from her chest.

"So, now that we're both sorry…" Monte began.

"I'm not sure, Monte. I just know that if we don't talk to

each other, then we've already lost. And—" Torie placed her right hand on Monte's knee "—I don't want to lose you. That much I do know," she said.

Monte didn't need to hear another word at the moment. As far as he was concerned, everything else could wait. He leaned forward, enveloping Torie in his arms and pulling her close to his chest.

"I missed you so much," he said.

"Me, too."

They sat holding each other for what felt like a sweet eternity. In that eternity there was no discord between them; there was only blossoming romance and carefree days and nights. It was Monte's ringing telephone that finally brought them back to the present.

"Look, you've got work to do. I didn't mean to barge in here and disrupt your day," Torie said, collecting herself. "I just couldn't take another minute of this."

"No, no, it's okay. I'm glad you came. We can't both be stubborn." Monte smiled.

"Do you want some company tonight?" Torie asked as she rose to leave.

"I'd love your company," Monte said.

Torie blushed. She leaned down, kissing Monte delicately on his lips.

"Why don't you pick me up on your way home. I've got a couple of things I want to give to Joshua and Josiah," she said.

Monte watched Torie depart. As he plowed through the rest of his day, he realized that the headache he'd been nursing for the past couple of days had dissipated. In its place were only positive images of his future. He held on to those pictures, hoping to will them into reality.

That night, with the boys sound asleep and his mother safely tucked into bed, Monte wasted no time making up for his immature behavior. He wanted to show Torie just how much she meant to him and also wanted her to think about what her nights on the west coast without him would be like.

Torie sat engrossed in the ten o'clock news and, when it was over, she realized that Monte had disappeared from the family room quite some time ago. She turned off the television and the lights and made her way to his bedroom. The door was closed and she wondered for a moment if he'd fallen asleep. She tapped lightly on the door twice.

"Come in," Monte called from the other side.

Torie turned the knob and pushed the door open slowly. Her eyes were met with a soft glow in an otherwise lightless room. She stepped inside and shut the door softly behind her. She stood there for a moment, taking it all in. So no wonder he had slipped away from her. Who had time for news when a scene for seduction needed to be set?

Fragrant votive candles were placed all around the room—on the dresser, on the headboard and on top of the armoire. A low fire burned in the fireplace. Monte lay on a comforter in front of the fire. He wore nothing but gray satin pajama pants that hugged his muscular lower body just enough to cause Torie's stomach muscles to contract. The fluffy goose-down pillows from his bed were also on the floor beside him. He'd set out a tray of white wine, fresh strawberries still wet from washing and a dish of Hershey's Kisses chocolate candy, already unwrapped and ready to be savored.

"I was wondering when you were going to come to bed," Monte said seductively.

"I would have come in here a whole lot sooner if I'd only known what was waiting for me." Torie smiled.

She walked slowly toward Monte, stopping when she reached the outskirts of the comforter. She pulled the black

T-shirt she wore over her head, tossing it to the floor beside her. She watched Monte's eyes widen as he took in her full C cups. She knew just what he was thinking and the thought of what he wanted to do to her breasts caused a sensuous moisture to form in her panties. She unbuttoned the low-rise jeans she wore and slid them down her legs. When she was free of them, she stood with one hand on her hip and, with the other, she freed her hair from the decorative comb that held it in place.

Monte swallowed. "Turn around," he demanded.

Torie obliged. She slowly did an about-face like an obedient soldier obeying a higher officer's command. Monte hissed when he saw that the round mounds that he loved to hold on to while she rode him were uninhibited, thanks to the thong she wore. Torie let him get an eyeful before turning slowly around again. She continued to stand, however, wanting Monte to ask for what he wanted.

"Come here," he ordered.

She bent slowly, dropping to her knees and then placing her hands on the comforter. She crawled the remainder of the way, her eyes never leaving his. Even in the darkness of the room, with just the glow from the fire and candles, she could see that he wore the expression of a starving man who would do anything for just one morsel of food. She planned on giving him enough to fill up every inch of his body and then some.

Monte picked up one of the strawberries and held it out in front of him. Torie reached him and opened her mouth to receive the fruit. Monte rubbed it along the outline of her lips before sticking it in the opening. Torie closed her mouth around the berry, but did not bite down on it. Instead, she gave it a firm suck and then released it. Monte's mouth fell open as he stared at her. Torie stuck out her tongue and licked the fruit in a circular motion. She let her tongue dance around its tip and then its entire circumference, before closing her mouth over it again. This time she bit down and removed a large chunk of the ripe berry. She moved closer to Monte with juice dripping down from her bottom lip. He leaned in, catching her mouth in his. They kissed and chewed until the strawberry was gone. They disengaged from their fiery kiss and Torie placed both hands on Monte's shoulders and pushed him backward until he was lying on his back. She swung her left leg over his body and straddled him. She sat down on his upper thighs and, though he tried to pull her up higher to make contact with his throbbing manhood, she wouldn't budge.

"Patience," she said.

Monte may have thought that this was his stage for seduction, but Torie had quickly flipped the script on him. She was in charge and he became a willing participant in her show. She leaned forward and kissed his face more than a dozen times, her soft lips brushing against his forehead, his nose, his cheeks—each one in turn—his chin and lips. She licked his jawline, tasting his masculine sweat. She felt him tremble beneath her as his hands cupped her behind and kneaded the flesh hungrily.

"Tor-ie, mmm," he breathed heavily.

Torie plucked a strawberry from the bowl and this time it was her turn to tease Monte's lips with the cool, wet fruit. When she finally allowed him to take it into his mouth, he ate it greedily, pretending it was her that he was devouring instead. Torie stuck a Hershey's Kiss in her own mouth and sucked on its sweetness for a moment before bending to find Monte's mouth. His coolness met her sweetness and both of their senses exploded from the combination. They tongued each other, slowly and deliciously at first, more ravenously as time wore on. Torie's breasts pressed against Monte's heaving chest. A fine sweat began to appear on her brow, her neck and down the center of her back. It was she who had grown impatient. Although the foreplay was sensuously mind-blowing, she wanted more—needed more.

She sat up, giving Monte room to remove his pants. His erection sprang from the material like an alert snake ready to release its venom. Suddenly, Torie changed her mind. She maneuvered so that her back faced Monte, her legs straddling his. She took him in her hands, felt him thicken as she stroked him tenderly. After several moments, her mouth took over where her hands left off. Monte writhed and moaned beneath her, his breathing ragged like an out-of-breath runner. As he begged for her to stop, then begged for her to never stop, she loved him with her lips and tongue, giving every inch an equal amount of attention.

Monte clawed at Torie's hips, pulling her legs from beneath her until she was no longer straddling, but lying on top of him, her gifts situated at eye level. From that point, it became a duel, a test of wills, as each sought to drive the other to the highest heights imaginable. Miniwaves of pleasure ripped through them individually, consecutively and then simultaneously, as if being transferred from one to another. They rested, gathering their strength, as they savored the insane gratification they'd reached, all the while wanting more.

Torie sat up and faced Monte. He picked up one of three condoms that lay next to the wine bottle. Torie watched as he tore the package open and rolled the latex down his shaft. She reached down to help him and then she took over, moving her hands up and down his pulsating member. He was ready and so was she.

When she lifted her waist, he positioned himself. She slid down deftly onto him and her waiting nest sang with satiating satisfaction. They moved together, in unison at times and in warring discord at others. They changed positions, finding ways to fill each other up. They called each other's names in musical harmony as their bodies rose to heights as yet unchartered. It was a long time before they came back to earth, and even when they did, they both felt surreal as if they had experienced an out-of-body event. Panting, Monte opened the chilled bottle of wine, poured a glass and took a long grateful sip. He then held the glass to Torie's parched lips as she wet her whistle. She collapsed against him and he released the now-empty glass. They lay for hours in the afterglow of their expression of love. In the wee hours of the morning, they made terrific use of the remaining two condoms, until neither had an ounce of strength left in them. In peaceful surrender, they slept until the sun peeked through the venetian blinds and kissed their tension-free bodies. Neither could predict what the future held for them and, for now, it didn't matter. All that mattered was that they'd found their way back to each other for the moment.

Chapter 19

Home at the Holidays

The Thanksgiving holiday brought a festive mood into the Lewis household. For the first time in the years without wife and mother, the Lewis men really felt like celebrating and giving thanks. With the help of Torie, a feast was prepared and the house was filled with holiday cheer. Monte donned his heavy sweater and fired up the electric deep fryer out on the back patio. Monte had not touched the fryer, a birthday gift from his wife, since she'd died. He made his signature fried turkey. He also baked a fresh ham, following one of Shawna's recipes.

Torie cooked collard greens the way she was taught as a young girl by her grandmother, a true Georgia peach, and she also made baked macaroni and cheese, black-eyed peas and buttermilk biscuits from scratch. To sweeten the menu up a little, Cheryl dropped off a pan of candied yams before heading to her eldest son's house for the day. All of the good food was made even better by the love and happiness around the table.

When Brenda Turner had first received her daughter's invitation to join her, her new boyfriend and his family for

Thanksgiving dinner, she'd considered declining. It wasn't that she didn't want to spend the holiday with her daughter. The fact of the matter was that Brenda did not approve of Torie getting involved with anyone again at this stage in her life. It was in direct contrast to what Torie had promised, and no matter how much she protested the contrary, Brenda was not entirely certain that Torie would not make the same mistakes she'd made in the past. Brenda was a woman who knew what a hefty price a woman could pay for the sake of love. She'd done it and there was no way that she'd sit back quietly and watch her only child do the same thing.

However, the holidays could be a lonely time. Darius and Sheila spent every other year with her parents in Seattle and, although they'd invited her along, she'd declined. Brenda considered the idea of staying at home alone, but the prospect of a quiet apartment and a table set for one depressed her terribly. The first-class flight Torie booked for her was also a contributing factor to her decision to come to New York. She turned out to be glad she did.

From the moment Brenda beheld Monte in person, she knew why her daughter had had such a hard time resisting him. Thirty minutes in his presence, and she knew why her daughter had fallen in love with him so quickly, despite her protests to the contrary. Brenda felt at ease in his home and at his table. Monte was a man who, unlike most of those Brenda had encountered in her life, was sure of himself and did not have a false bone in his body. The confidence he exuded was contagious and his good-hearted nature made people feel as though he genuinely cared about them. Brenda was no exception.

The final gold star in Brenda's book was the two well-mannered, delightful little boys Monte was raising on his own. They amused the adults with stories about school escapades and silly knock-knock jokes. They helped set the table and carry out the covered entrées. They called Brenda "ma'am" and kept offering to do things for her. After dinner, Joshua loaded the dishes that Josiah handed to him in the dishwasher, while Monte cleared the table and stored the leftover food into the refrigerator. When Monte finally told them to get washed up and ready for bed, they did so without protest. They kissed both Torie and Brenda good-night, went in to see their grandmother, who had not been up to eating at the table with them, and went to their rooms in good cheer. That was truly a testament, Brenda knew, to their upbringing.

Later that night, while Torie drove them back to the city in Monte's car, Brenda had nothing but nice things to say about Monte. However, her reservations about the romance had not been entirely put to rest.

"How long ago did you say Monte lost his wife?" Brenda asked.

"It's been a little over three years."

"Cancer, I'd bet. With all the money we spend on weapons and space exploration—and nonsense—you'd think the government would pour more money into medical research. People shouldn't still be dying from cancer in this day and age."

"I don't know if it was cancer or not. Apparently, she wasn't sick very long before she passed," Torie answered.

"Oh. Well, I'd bet a hundred bucks it was cancer. My neighbor Paige lost her daughter to cancer last year, did I tell you? Only forty years old—brain cancer. That's such an awful way to die," Brenda lamented.

"Mama, please don't be morbid." Torie sighed.

"I'm sorry, but it is. And for those little boys to have to go through that, it's a shame. Those sweet little boys. Did you see that Joshua? He's like a little man, offering me a cup of tea or coffee to go with my pie. He's too cute. Ooh, and Josiah... don't you just want to eat him up?" Brenda laughed.

Brenda leaned her head back against the seat and closed her eyes, feeling the effects of all the food she'd eaten plus the two glasses of wine she'd consumed.

"They are great little boys. They make their father proud," Torie agreed.

"Humph, it's too bad Monte's mother is fairing so poorly. I know that can't be easy for him. And she's young, too. She's only a few years older than me. Thank God my health has been okay, praise Jesus. And my mind ain't in such bad shape, either," Brenda said.

Torie nodded in agreement on both accounts. She knew that Mrs. Lewis's illness was taking a toll on Monte. She didn't know how she'd handle a similarly debilitating illness in her own mother. Every day Monte tried to sound hopeful, but she could tell that he was losing that battle. Although Mrs. Lewis had been having some not so bad days, it was becoming obvious that the Alzheimer's disease was not going to release its grip on her. All Torie could do was be supportive when Monte wanted to talk about it, and be patient when he didn't.

Brenda fell soundly asleep by the time they'd reached the Southern State Parkway. Her light snoring made Torie smile. She was glad that her mother had had a good holiday, and she also sent up a special thank-you to the Man upstairs for allowing Brenda and Monte to get along so well. Torie knew from their first conversation about Monte, and the dozen or so they'd had since, that Brenda disapproved of Torie getting serious with anyone right now. She glanced over at her sleeping mother and shook her head. It didn't matter how old Torie got—she apparently would never be too old for her mother to try to run her life.

Brenda awoke early the next morning, well rested and in good spirits. Torie heard her mother clunking around in the kitchen. She lay in bed for a while, enjoying the sounds of her mother preparing breakfast. She felt like a little kid again, back at home, and she awaited the call that would come from Brenda when breakfast was finally ready.

"Torie," Brenda called about twenty minutes later.

Torie kicked back the covers, slipped on a red silk bathrobe and stepped out into the hallway.

"Be right there, Mama," she called before heading into the bathroom.

Torie emerged a few minutes later to find her mother seated at a table laden with fresh coffee, hominy grits, sunny-side eggs and turkey bacon. Torie's mouth watered as she sat down.

"Mmm, I haven't had hominy grits in ages. You know I can never cook them just right," Torie said as she sprinkled pepper on her eggs.

"That's because you always try to cook them too fast. I've told you before—I don't care what the box says, grits need to simmer for a long time," Brenda said.

The women enjoyed a relaxing breakfast. Afterward, as Torie refilled the coffee cups, Brenda seized the opportunity to speak her piece.

"Torie, I really like Monte. I do. And his boys. I had a great time yesterday," she began.

Torie felt the *but* coming; however, she was not about to fall into her mother's trap.

"I'm glad, Mama," she replied casually.

Brenda pursed her lips, choosing her next words carefully. "I wouldn't be saying anything at all if I didn't think you needed to hear it. I can tell by the way you two interact that this thing has moved far beyond casual like you made it out to be. Are you in love with that man?"

"Yes, Mama, I am," Torie said without hesitation. "I'm in love with him and with his boys. And before you even go there, let's not. I know exactly what you're going to say and, believe me, it's nothing I haven't already said to myself. However, it's different this time, Mama. I'm not a young and naive little girl. My eyes are wide open, and I know what I'm doing."

"Do you?"

"Yes, I do. Monte is nothing like Kevin was. He's nothing like any man I've ever known. He celebrates my independence and supports me in my goals."

"That's great, honey," Brenda said.

She spooned a little more sugar into her coffee cup. She stirred slowly, watching the sweetener dissolve before speaking again.

"I've always admired your optimism, Torie. You've had some tough breaks in life, but you always seem to land on your feet. Always got that bright smile and those positive thoughts. It's a good quality to have," Brenda said, looking at her daughter. "But, honey, you've got to consider that you and Monte may not be looking at this thing realistically. You're headed to the other side of the country to work on that television show. Monte has roots here. He's got those boys to think of. He's got his ailing mother to care for. He can't just zip out to California on a whim, and you need to focus on your career. You can't come flying back to the east coast when you're missing each other."

"What are you saying, Mama? That we can't be together because we'll be living in different states? Mama, people find ways to make long-distance romances work all the time. And besides, this is only temporary."

Torie cringed to hear her mother giving voice to the very concerns that had caused her so much angst over the past few weeks. There was no way, however, that Torie was going to let Brenda know how worried she was.

"You don't know that," Brenda was saying. "Did you ever stop to think about what comes after the show? Your career is about to take off. There could be movies, jobs that might take you out of the country. You never know," Brenda continued excitedly.

"Of course I've thought about that, Mama. Aren't I the one who told you that my career was moving forward? You wanted me to stick to little off-the-beaten-path plays and commercials, lest you forget."

"No, I didn't forget, and I still don't think you should completely discount the vehicles that got you this far. However, I ain't too proud to say that you were right. You took a chance, and it paid off. I'm proud of you, honey."

"I know you are, Mama, but I really don't think you truly understand how hard I've worked for this, and that I'm going to continue to work hard to reach the highest levels of professional success that I can. I've thought about all of that."

"And have you talked it over with Monte?"

"Yes…somewhat. Mama, I won't lie. I was very concerned about this relationship, especially in the beginning. For a minute I began to doubt myself, doubt my ability to focus on loving Monte and doing what I needed to do for myself and my career. But, Mama, why can't I have it all? If I just believe that I can, if I stay strong and focused, why can't I?"

"I used to think having it all was possible, but, sweetie, life just…life doesn't always …" Brenda trailed off as she looked at her daughter.

"As long as Monte supports me and my goals, I think we can make it work. At least, I know it's worth a try," Torie said softly.

Brenda reached over and patted Torie's hand.

"I hope you're right about that, Torie," Brenda said after a short pause.

"Mama, please just be happy for me."

Each woman settled into their private thoughts as silence fell between them. Although they held different levels of optimism, a nagging doubt plagued them both.

Chapter 20

Hello Hollywood

"*Chica*, did you get references for this couple you're subletting to?" Lisette asked.

With a purple marker, Lisette labeled the brown cardboard box she'd just sealed with duct tape.

"Yes, I did. I got a letter from her employer and from his previous landlord in Boston. They moved here for him to complete his graduate studies at NYU. So you can relax, Ms. Worrywart. I've covered all the bases," Torie said.

She wiped the moisture that had begun accumulating on her forehead with the back of her hand before picking up the next glass-framed photograph from the stack on the floor beside her. She tore off a sheet of bubble wrap from a roll and began covering the picture.

"I'm just checking. You never know. I'd hate for you to come back and find your apartment destroyed or, worse, find those people up in here with fifteen of their relatives from back home." Lisette laughed.

"You're nuts. It'll be okay. I've given them a six-month lease and told them that we'll see what happens after that."

"Hmm, I see," Lisette replied. After a brief pause, she

asked, "Is that the same thing you said to Monte?" she asked.

Lisette eyed her girl suspiciously. Torie had not said much about the status of her relationship with Monte in the past few weeks and Lisette had fallen back, thinking that Torie would eventually open up about it. Lisette imagined that the impending separation could not be easy for Torie to deal with, but she was also proud of her girl for staying the course when it came to pursuing her professional goals.

Torie smiled. "Monte won't hear of it. He keeps saying things like it's all going to work out and three thousand miles ain't nothing. Says he loves me and wants me to live my dreams. If that means waiting one month or a hundred months, that's what he's going to do. He's talking good talk, but I guess the test will be in the doing, huh?"

"Amen to that. Like my papi used to say to his customers, *nosotros hablamos cuando la oficina de cambio.*"

"Say what?"

"Loosely translated, it means, 'let's talk about it when the check clears.' It's, like, people talk a good game and make all kinds of promises, but as we all know, talk does not pay the bills. You feel me?"

Lisette and Torie laughed, their fists bumping in agreement. Every day Torie soaked in a little more of Monte's optimism, allowing it to nourish her heart and soul and keep her fears at bay. She knew it wouldn't be easy, but she also knew that she wanted him to be right. The thought of losing out on love again was one that she didn't relish. Especially given the fact that, with Monte, it felt as if she'd found her soul mate for the first time.

"Hey, I'm really proud of you. I know I give you a hard time some of the time—"

"All of the time," Torie teased.

"Whatever. Anyway, you're really making me proud, little sister," Lisette said.

"Aww, don't make me cry. I promised myself I was going to get through this move without turning into waterworks," Torie said.

"No, we're not going to cry. This is a time of celebration. My girl is going off to do the damned thing and I couldn't be happier. But I want you to know how proud I am of you. You could have given up after what happened last year. Or you could have done the same thing this time and let your chance slip through your fingers," Lisette said.

"Oh, like you would have let that happen?"

"Okay, on second thought, maybe not. But still, I'm proud of you, with your bad, independent self."

Torie crawled across the carpet between them and threw both arms around Lisette's neck.

"Thank you, girl, for always having my back," Torie said as she hugged her friend.

"You're welcome. Now go out there to *Follywood* and give them hell."

"Miss Torie, Torie…did you have a good flight?" Martin called as he scooped Torie into his arms and gave her a tight squeeze.

"Hey, Martin," Torie said, hugging him back and then releasing him and taking a small step backward. "The flight was pretty good, I must say. No turbulence, no crying babies and the salmon they served wasn't half-bad."

Martin held on to Torie's shoulders as they laughed. When he finally released her, he reached down and took the carry-on bag she had.

"Well, then, it's all good. Why don't we go and get your bags," Martin said.

He took Torie by the hand and led her through the crowded

airport. Mid-January was still considered holiday travel time and, judging by the steady throng of people milling about, Bob Hope Airport seemed to Torie to be a major hub.

"Martin, I really appreciate you coming to pick me up and for helping me land an apartment in your building and, well, for everything. You've been terrific," Torie said, looking up at Martin.

They were standing on the right side of the moving walkway, but they were not walking. Other travelers passed them by on the left, in a hurry to get to their destinations.

"How many times are you going to thank me and how many times am I going to tell you it was really no big deal? There was no way I was going to let a Southern gal like you relocate to my neck of the woods without a personal escort."

"Be that as it may, I really do appreciate it. So have you spoken to Lana or Robert?"

"Yep. Rob called me yesterday when he got in. He's got some friends who live down in Pasadena so he's staying with them for a while. He said he wasn't sure where he wanted to live just yet so he was going to hang out with them until he found something he liked. To be honest, I think he's afraid that his role on the show might be short-lived."

"Shoot, the same could be said for all of us. We've still got to make homes for ourselves."

"I hear you. And Lana, well, you know that girl. She's been here for two weeks and she's already met some guy. Suffice it to say, she hasn't had much time to holla—well, at least not at me, if you know what I mean."

"Ooh, you're terrible, Martin. As long as she makes time for our little bitty show, then she can do whatever she wants. All I know is that I've come out here with my game face on and everybody else's better be on, too, if we're going to make this show number one in it's time slot!" Torie stated emphatically.

"I know that's right. Man, some days I have to pinch myself to be sure that this is all really happening. And the fact that we're shooting out here in Cali is icing on an already scrumptious cake. I can't tell you how happy my mama is to have me back within thirty minutes of her."

"Yeah, well, I don't know about all that. I was just really getting used to New York and now I'm starting all over again by myself," Torie said.

She didn't want to sound as though she was complaining. She knew that this was the chance of a lifetime and she was truly grateful. But as she watched the descent onto the tarmac at Bob Hope, the realization that not only had she left behind snow and twenty-degree temperatures but also said goodbye to the most important people in her life hit home. Lisette, Monte, Josiah, Joshua and her mother were now three thousand miles on the other side of the country and she might as well have taken a trip to the moon for as close as she felt to them just then.

"Don't worry, T., I'll play stand-in. By the time I finish showing you my Cali, you won't be homesick at all," Martin said with a warm smile.

Torie looped her arm through his as they stepped off the moving walkway and hugged it close to her. Martin had already proven to be a really good friend. She resolved that dwelling on her melancholy thoughts and weighing him down with her tales of woe-is-me would be disrespectful to all that he'd done for her. She planted a smile on her face and continued on to the baggage-claim area.

Like a kid in a candy store, Torie sat with her face practically pressed to the glass of Martin's convertible. She wished that they could ride with the top down, but it had begun to rain as soon as they pulled out of the parking lot. As they sped along the I-5, passing breathtaking valleys and vast mountainous terrain, Torie finally felt as though she understood why easterners would be willing to trade in their skyscrapers and move west.

"God, this is so beautiful," Torie squealed.

"Okay, you're really looking like a tourist now," Martin said when Torie pulled out the digital camera that Monte had given her as a going-away present.

"Can you believe this is my first digital camera? Monte gave it to me a couple of days ago. I was still using my old Olympus camera and taking rolls of film to the drugstore like a square," Torie said, laughing at herself.

"Good old Monte. How is he?" Martin asked.

"He's excellent, thank you. He and the boys drove me to the airport this morning."

Snap…snap. Torie took pictures of the Saint Bernard that was riding in the car next to them with his head sticking out of the window. He was moving his tongue up and down, seeming to be trying to lap at the air.

"Boys? How many kids does he have?" Martin asked.

"Two. Joshua is nine and Josiah is seven. Joshua's got a birthday coming up next month—double digits—so he's feeling a little mature these days." Torie smiled. "And little Josiah's front tooth is finally growing in. He was beginning to get a little self-conscious because all the kids in his class have their permanents already, at least in front."

Torie continued snapping pictures as she caught a glimpse of Toluca Lake.

"Wow, that's, uh…well, I'm a little surprised to hear you talk like that," Martin said.

"Like what?" she asked.

"Like, I don't know, motherly. I didn't know that you and Monte were, well, as close as all that. Sounds like you're one big happy family," Martin said dryly.

Torie considered Martin's statement before replying. He was right to a certain extent. She did feel like Monte and the boys were family to her. She prayed for them before she prayed for herself. She enjoyed listening to them all talk about their days when they were apart and she liked making plans for them when they were together. Even though she'd always thought little girls' clothing and accessories were much cuter, she'd begun to enjoy going to the boy's section in stores and picking up things for them. And by the time she'd finished hugging and kissing Joshua and Josiah the night before she left New York, her cheeks were wet and mascara stained.

"Well, I'm not their mother. I like to think of myself as a really good friend to them…or an auntie. I mean, they're the best little boys in the world, and trust me, I'm not just saying that," she stated.

"And what about their dad? Is he the best big boy in your world?"

"Funny," Torie said, snapping a picture of Martin.

"Hey, knock it off. I get paid for this face now or hadn't you heard?" he joked.

They pulled off of San Fernando Boulevard and into a circular driveway of a sand-colored three-story building. He stopped the car and turned toward Torie.

"We're home," he said.

"Really? Ooh, this is nice." Torie beamed as she got out of the car.

She closed the door and then spun in a complete circle, taking in all that there was to see. The rain had turned into a light drizzle and the late-afternoon sun peeked through gray clouds. A doorman stepped out from behind his desk and helped Martin carry Torie's three large suitcases inside.

"This looks like a hotel," Torie said of the brightly decorated lobby with its potted palm trees and pale marble floors.

"What've you got in here, the kitchen sink?" Martin asked as he trudged behind her.

"I'll have you know that I left quite a bit behind. My best

friend, Lisette, is storing most of my things," Torie called over her shoulder.

"Women," Martin muttered under his breath.

They took a short ride in an elevator that was paneled with mirrors on all sides. Stepping out on the third floor, Torie again remarked at how beautiful the place was. By the time Martin opened the door to unit C1, Torie's new home, she had run out of words. The apartment was light and airy. The bare parquet floors shown brilliantly and there was a huge bay window that spanned one side of the living room. The only furniture was a plain beige sofa, a dinette and the queen sleigh bed Torie had ordered and had had delivered the week before. The kitchen was large and spacious, complete with stainless-steel appliances and a breakfast nook.

"Oh, Martin, this place is so nice. I can't believe the rent is so cheap."

"Yeah, it beats the hell out of New York, that's for sure. I was going broke out there."

Torie crossed to the window and looked down onto the grounds. To the left there was a tennis court, to the right a Grecian-shaped swimming pool and lawn chairs. A playground bordered the pool area to the right. Finally, she could glimpse the busy boulevard teeming with shops that she couldn't wait to visit.

"Martin, I know I've already told you this, but I really appreciate all of your help," Torie said.

She walked over to Martin and gave him a tight hug.

"Now, I don't want to you to feel like you have to babysit me. I'm sure you've got a million better things to do."

Torie guided Martin toward the door, her arm looped through his.

"No, I really don't have anything better to do than to help my favorite actress get settled," Martin said.

"Oh, stop. You know Gabrielle Union is your favorite actress. Get on out of here so I can get settled."

"All right, but give me a call tomorrow so I can show you around town before we have to head in for rehearsals. I've set the rest of the week aside just for you."

Torie closed the door behind Martin and leaned against it, soaking it all in. The sparsely furnished living room echoed with the sound of her heels clicking across the parquet floors. She stepped out onto the balcony to find that the rain had picked up once again. She stared out over the swimming pool below her, watching as the rain pelted the water's surface and caused it to ripple in little waves. She closed her eyes and imagined warmer, sunny weather and saw herself lying out on one of the lawn chairs, soaking up a little sun. She'd close her eyes and hear the laughter of Josiah and Joshua as they splashed about in the pool. Monte would be lying on the chair next to her, reading a book or listening to his iPod handheld. It'd be the first of many visits and they'd all be having a ball.

Torie opened her eyes to the rain and dark skies. She shook her head from side to side, refusing to let herself become glum again. She needed cheering up and she knew just the trick. She glanced at the clock and accounted for the time difference. Three-thirty west coast time meant that it was six-thirty back in New York. Monte and the boys would have finished eating Sunday dinner and would be watching football, working on a school project or playing video games. She pulled her cell phone out of her purse at hit the speed dial.

"Hey, Cali, what's happening?" Monte said, answering on the first ring.

"Hi, babe," Torie exclaimed.

Just the sound of Monte's voice catapulted her up from down in the dumps.

"Are you getting drunk yet from all that sunshine?"

"Uh, well, considering it's been raining since I got here, I'd say that was a big fat no!"

"What? I thought it never rained in sunny California," Monte joked.

"Yeah, well, I hate to tell you but while that song says it never rains in *Southern* California, Burbank must not have gotten the memo. How're you doing?"

"I'm great. The boys and I went to see that new robot movie this afternoon. I think Josiah ate too much popcorn because he knocked out as soon as we got home without eating dinner."

"Aww," Torie said, imagining Josiah's goofy ear-to-ear grin being covered in butter and salt.

"What about you? Was the flight okay?"

"It was long, but otherwise it was fine."

"Oh, and was, uh, your friend Martin there on time to pick you up?" Monte asked stiffly.

Torie knew that Monte was not pleased about the fact that Martin was the person helping her get settled. She agreed that Martin could be a little over the top at times and sometimes he came on a little strong, but he was perfectly harmless, she'd assured Monte.

"Yes, and he was a perfect gentleman. Oh, Monte, this apartment is gorgeous. The photos on their Web site didn't do it justice. I've got a nice view of the back of the property—the pool, tennis courts and grounds. And it's so spacious. I can't believe I'm paying a third less than what I was paying in Manhattan and have twice as much space," Torie boasted.

"I believe you. Anywhere outside of Manhattan gives you more for the money. So, babe, it's back to rehearsals tomorrow, huh?"

"Yep, first thing in the morning we'll be trying to pull this thing together. Martin's going to give me a ride to the studio, but I'm definitely planning to get to a car dealership within the next week or so. I can't keep relying on him to take me back and forth to work every day," Torie said.

"I'll say."

"And besides, I want to be able to just get up and go, you know? Explore this town on my own a little," Torie finished, ignoring Monte's meaningful second to her motion. "Ooh, maybe I'll get a cute little convertible so I can ride with the top down, wind blowing through my hair—"

"All right, watch it now. Don't turn Hollywood on me!" Monte laughed.

They talked for another half an hour while Torie unpacked two of her three suitcases. She picked out a pair of lightweight gray wool slacks and a pink cotton sweater for her first day at the studio. She began running a hot bath after she'd scoured the tub. She added bath salts before, reluctantly, she and Monte said their good-nights.

"I wish I was there to scrub your back," he said softly.

"Mmm, in my mind you will be," Torie replied devilishly.

"On that note, let me go and hop into my tub, too." Monte laughed. "Good night, babe. Sweet dreams."

"You, too," Torie replied.

"And break a leg tomorrow."

Less than thirty minutes went by before Torie settled into a tub of bubbles and hot water. She'd lit two of the sandalwood candles she'd managed to find in one of her suitcases and had selected a playlist on her iPod that consisted of all of her favorite love ballads. She closed her eyes and floated to one of the happiest places her mind could take her—back to Monte's arms. She pictured his hands on her, running her own up and down her inner thighs as his had just a few hours ago. She squeezed her legs together and wrapped her arms around her body tightly, wanting to capture the memory of his body against hers and hold it there forever. She didn't know how long she could go without feeling his touch, seeing his face or just inhaling the scent of him, and it was that thought that plagued her for the rest of her first night in her new life.

Chapter 21

Missing You

Two weeks into Torie's absence Monte began to feel as if he would truly lose his mind. He found himself wide-awake in the middle of the night when he should have been sleeping, and half-asleep in the middle of the day when he should have been working. Twice he was so busy daydreaming that he put flour in his coffee instead of sugar, and yesterday, he drove all the way to the office with the car's air conditioner on full blast. When he got there, it took some time before he realized why his teeth were chattering.

He was so distracted at work with thoughts of Torie that he decided that he needed to take a few days off. He found himself reading the same passages in contracts over and over again, and still not being able to grasp the meaning of what he read. He decided he'd do some things around the house while the boys were at school and be there to get them off the bus.

Late one morning Monte sat reading the newspaper by his mother's bedside. The boys were in school and the nurse was seated in the den having a cup of coffee. Marva had not been talking much of late and Monte felt as though she were slipping a bit further away from this world with each setting sun. He felt as powerless as he had when he was a child and he'd watched her sit at the kitchen table, holding her head in her hands as she pored through the stacks of bills in front of her. He'd wanted to make her feel better. He'd try to get her to laugh, by telling jokes or making funny faces. She'd smile absently and then tell him to go to his room and read a book.

Life had been difficult for them, but Monte remembered somehow feeling as though it would all be okay. Even when they'd had to eat grits and gravy for breakfast every day for weeks, his mother would rub the top of his head and tell him that as long as their bellies were full that's all that mattered. She'd tell him that God would make a way for them and he believed her. He also promised her and himself that one day he'd make sure they had everything they could possibly want. Marva would kiss his forehead and tell him that all he had to do was make sure they had what they needed, nothing more.

Monte was a diligent student, making honor roll through grade school, receiving awards in high school and landing a full scholarship to Hampton University in Virginia. His mother had been so proud of him, bragging to everyone at work and at church. He aimed to keep his promise to her and he thought that he'd have years to spoil her the way some man should have.

Monte looked at his mother now, resting against the pillows he'd fluffed beneath her moments before. Her hair was still more pepper than black and, although she'd lost weight, her skin still held traces of its former youthful beauty. He felt cheated, as though time had played a cruel trick on him. He'd wanted to see her spend her golden years traveling the world and doing all the things that she'd never been able to afford as she'd raised him. Although Monte forced himself to accept the fact that it wasn't going to happen, that acceptance did not make the pain lessen by any degree.

"Oh, Mama," he whispered.

Her eyes fluttered open and, for a moment, they were cloudy and disoriented. When she came to rest on Monte's face, he automatically braced himself. He never knew when she would recognize him.

"Monte? Baby, what you doing here? Why aren't you at work?" she said.

He smiled broadly, glad that she was in the present with him even if it couldn't last.

"I took a few days off to do some things around the house. And," he said, picking up one of her thin hands from the bed, "to spend some time with my best girl."

"Best girl? Boy, please. I haven't been a girl in years." Marva laughed, patting Monte's hand. "Besides, you know that pretty young thing's got your attention."

"Who, Torie? Aww, she's all right, but she can't hold a candle to you."

"Ooh, you're silly. How are you two doing?"

"Well, you know how it is, Mama," Monte said lightly.

"No, I don't know. Why don't you tell me how it is? Are you happy, Monte?"

"Yes, ma'am, I am. I love her. She's…she's fantastic. And the boys love her, too."

"So what's the problem?"

"I don't know. I guess I'm just a worrywart like you always said. I want to make her happy, but I'm not sure if I can. She's got her career, and she's at a place where things are really about to start happening for her. That's great and all, believe me, but—"

"But you're worried about whether or not there's room in her life for you and her work?"

Monte nodded, amazed at his mother's unrelenting ability to read between the lines of what he said, even now.

"Monte, I don't know what to say about that. But I will tell you something that I think you need to hear. You and those boys done had your share of heartache and it's about time you had some happiness. If this girl makes you happy, then you'd better do whatever you have to do to hold on to that. You hear me?"

"Yes, ma'am."

"Good. 'Cause I ain't going to be around forever and this house needs a woman in it."

Monte laughed, agreeing wholeheartedly with his mother's testament. He leaned back in the chair and just sat in silence at his mother's side. Like most kids, he used to cringe when his mother attempted to give him advice, believing that she couldn't possibly understand what he was going through at the time. He sent a silent prayer up to heaven, thanking God for at least one more opportunity for his mother to share her wisdom with him. It felt good knowing that the person who knew him best and wanted nothing but good things for him supported him in this way. He didn't doubt that the separation from Torie would be rough, but he also couldn't stand the thought of being without her.

His mother's words stuck in his head and he repeated them over and over again. *This house needs a woman in it.* He couldn't argue with that statement, but he wondered if Torie was, in fact, that woman. Yes, she was beautiful, exciting, intelligent and caring. She was great with the boys and was the kind of woman who made his heart skip a beat at the thought of just talking to her. And while that added up to a great deal of good, it didn't necessarily make two. The question was whether she could fit into his lifestyle and the life that he wanted for his children. Monte sighed the hundredth of a million sighs to come. Only time would tell if they were meant to be, and all he could hope was that the chips were stacked in their favor.

Chapter 22

On My Mind

"I just called to tell you that I really don't know if I'm going to be able to wait until your flight gets in tomorrow. I might just hop on the red-eye and meet you at the airport in New York," Torie breathed excitedly into the telephone.

"I miss you, too, baby," Monte said. He took a swing at the air in front of him, trying to find the right words to deliver news that would undoubtedly devastate Torie.

"Ooh, Monte, I can't wait until you get here so I can show you all around my little town. Tomorrow night, we'll have dinner at Bella Vista's, which is in the downtown Burbank area. They make the best penne with clam sauce you've ever had. Sounds good, huh?"

"Yeah, it sounds great. But, Torie—"

"And in the morning we'll drive out to Roscoe's in L.A. and have some chicken and waffles. I've only been out there once because that stuff is addictive. I'll mess around and move up two dress sizes before I can say Jenny Craig diet." Torie laughed. "Will you still love me when I'm fat?"

"Of course. I'll love you if you gain six hundred pounds and have to be lifted out of bed with a crane," Monte joked.

"Okay, now you're going too far. Anyway, I've got a bunch of less fattening activities planned for us, as well. Make sure you bring your running sneakers because I've found the most beautiful trail and, oh, there's a festival going on in town on Saturday. And bring a suit because we've got that lounge opening to go to on Thursday. I told you about it, right?"

"Torie," Monte interrupted, raising his voice. "I'm not coming."

"What? What did you say, Monte?" Torie asked hesitantly.

Monte did not answer right away, the line tense with the silence. Monte wished he could make those seconds stretch into hours, but there was no reprieve, no easy escape route for him.

"I can't come. Believe me, baby, I really want to. Up until this morning, I was all set to come. But—"

"But what? We've been planning this for weeks. You said everything was all set with the boys and your mother. What's the problem? Is it work?"

The disappointment in Torie's voice rang clearly through the phone lines, gripping Monte's heartstrings. He hated to be the source of any disappointment or sadness in Torie's life, yet he seemed to be in that position more often than not. He considered lying for a split second, blaming some client crisis for his last-minute bailout. However, that second was short-lived for Monte as he was not a man who could comfortably dress himself in a lie, no matter how inconvenient the truth.

"Tomorrow is Shawna's birthday," Monte said.

The line was silent as Torie absorbed the weight of Monte's words. He waited for a response that would signify some understanding.

"Torie?" Monte called finally.

"I'm here."

"Listen, I know this is messed up and, believe me, I really intended to come. It's just that—"

"No, Monte, you don't have to explain. I understand," Torie said shortly.

"You do? I mean, I...I'm glad. I miss you so much baby," Monte said.

"Look, I've gotta go."

"Go? Wait, I don't want to hang up without explaining things to you. You see, Josiah—"

"No, Monte, really, you've said enough. Uh, you have a good night, Monte, and tell the boys I said hello."

Before Monte could respond, Torie hung up the receiver. He sat in disbelief at the sound of the click in his ear, followed by a harsh busy signal and a recorded voice advising him that if he'd like to make a call, he would need to hang up and dial a number. Monte released the call and pressed Torie's name in the speed dial. When her voice rang out asking him to leave a message at the beep, he regretted for the first time in his life his penchant for telling the truth.

Chapter 23

Opposing Forces

"Monte, please, let's not make this any harder than it already is," Torie said.

She folded a T-shirt and placed it in the overnight bag that was open on her bed. Her flight to Atlanta was scheduled for departure in a few hours and she'd need to head out to the airport shortly. The past three days had delivered an anguish that neither of them knew how to deal with. However, their reality was one that could not be denied.

"I'm not trying to make it harder, baby. I just think we need to take the time to talk…to figure some things out."

Monte took a pair of jeans from the laundry table and folded them. He'd been doing the kids' laundry when, on a whim, he'd dialed Torie's number again. He'd called a dozen times in the past few days and she'd answered only once before, speaking long enough to tell him that she didn't feel like talking and needed some space.

"Torie, I love you," he said now, wanting Torie to get out of her head for just a moment and into her heart. That was the part of her where he knew that he still resided.

"And you know that I love you, too, Monte. But we both realize that love's not enough."

"Since when? Since I canceled one trip out to see you? Come on, Torie, you're not being fair."

Monte dropped the jeans onto the folding table and leaned against the dryer. The anxiety he'd been feeling for the past few days was building up, threatening to explode.

"I'm not being fair? Don't you dare say that to me, Monte. I've been nothing but fair and honest with you. I told you from the beginning what my fears are and you promised that you could and would do whatever it takes to make me feel like I'm not going too far with you."

"I'm not trying to go back on that promise, Torie, but come on. Do you really think I'm not risking anything here? You're not the only one who is scared."

"Funny, you seemed to have all the answers a few months ago."

Torie opened and shut dresser drawers, forgetting what she was searching for. She plopped down on the bed beside her bag and held her head in her hands.

"Torie, I don't know everything. I just feel that, despite the pain and loss I've suffered through, I've moved on...with you."

"You're starting to sound like you're regretting that."

"Regret? Never. I don't regret one minute that I've spent with you." Monte ran his hand roughly down his face, his frustration causing him to tremble. "I don't know Torie... maybe you were right. Maybe we rushed this. I love you and that's all I could see, all I could think about."

Torie's eyes filled with tears as she braced herself to listen to the words that deep down inside she'd been expecting to hear all along.

"My boys lost their mother, the woman who gave them life and nurtured them. I thought I could love them through that.

I thought I could teach them to cherish Shawna's memory as they grew and to move on. Maybe it was too fast for them to forget exactly what they'd lost in her. When her birthday came this year, Josiah was more upset than he'd been for the past three years. And then Josh— Anyway, I just couldn't leave them."

"Monte, you were right to stay with your boys. I understand that and, trust me, I'm not angry about why you canceled the trip. But it also made me realize that you and your sons have a life, a history that I am not a part of."

"That's just it, Torie. We have a history that had some really good times in it and ended unexpectedly. We also have a future, and I want to give them the best future possible."

"And I want that for you all."

"Torie, you are a part of that future—at least, I want you to be. I just think that if I'm going to ask my boys to move on, I have to know that this is permanent."

"Permanent? What are you saying, Monte?"

Monte wished he could look into Torie's eyes and have his fears soothed by the beauty and love that he knew rested there. He felt his nerves grow shaky and he swallowed the fear that rose in his throat, threatening to hold on to his words. He'd thought about this moment for the past three days and had worked up his courage little by little. Time had almost run out and he knew that this was the chance for him to step up.

"I'm saying that I know how hard you've worked to get to this point in your career, and I want you to reach that star you've been working toward. I want to be there by your side when you take to the red carpet or win awards."

Torie lifted one quivering hand to her mouth.

"Torie, I want you to be a part of my and the boys' lives for as long as God grants us. Now, I'm not asking you to take Shawna's place—it would be unfair to everyone involved to expect that. I'm asking you, Torie Turner, to make a commitment to me, to the boys. Will you marry me?"

"Marry...marry you?" Torie stammered.

Certainly, she'd heard him wrong. She waited for him to tell her that she had not heard what her ears thought they had.

"Yes, marry me," he repeated.

"Monte, I...I don't know what to say. Wow, this is... I didn't expect this."

"I know I didn't exactly plan this. It should have been done in person, and I don't have a ring or anything, but I promise you, I'll get you one. The biggest diamond your hand can hold. Don't worry about that,"

"No, Monte, it's not about the ring or— Monte, this is out of left field," Torie said.

She stood abruptly and walked away from the bed. She stopped in front of the chest of drawers in the corner of the room. She felt trapped in her own bedroom.

"Is it? Is it really that much of a shock to you? Torie, you know how I feel. I've been honest with you from the start. I know getting with a man who has a ready-made family wasn't what you were looking for, but it happened. You can't deny what we mean to each other. You love me, don't you?"

"Yes, Monte. I do love you. I love everything about you, and I love those boys, too. But, Monte, marriage is a big deal. It's a commitment that affects every aspect of a person's life. I mean, it's not something you do on the spur of the moment," Torie said.

"I'm not asking you to marry me right now...today. I just want us to make the commitment to build this relationship up, push it forward. I want to know that we're committed to each other...to this relationship and to doing everything in our power to make it last. We'll work out all the details later. In a few months, when the show stops taping, you'll come home to New York and we'll plan. I'm sure you'll want to have a big wedding and that's fine. We can do it however you want to do it. Just so long as you promise me that one day soon you'll wear my ring and be my wife. Be a mother to my boys."

Monte paced the room, waiting for her answer. He wished so hard that he could pull her into his arms, kiss her and love her until she had no doubts about the depth of his feelings for her.\

But Torie did understand how much love he felt, because she felt it, too. It was precisely that knowledge that made his proposal feel like a knife through her heart. She was so torn, wanting to make him happy but at the same time feeling as if she was being backed into a corner and there was no easy way out.

"Monte," she began.

Tears sprang in Torie's eyes. At the sound of the quaver in her voice, the smile slowly faded on Monte's face. The tone of her voice told him that he was not going to get the answer that he'd wanted. He hadn't even considered that possibility and was not prepared for it.

"Monte, I can't…not right now. I can't make that kind of a commitment to you, and it wouldn't be fair for me to let you think we're headed for something that I'm just not sure about yet. Monte—"

"Please, Torie. Please, just trust me, trust us. We can make this work."

"No, Monte," she said firmly.

Monte stumbled backward, feeling as though he'd just been punched in the gut. He struggled to get air into his lungs and fought to maintain his composure. He rubbed his jaw roughly as his mind churned with thoughts that made him feel as if he were on fire. It was more than the rejection. At that moment, he felt, as if by saying no, Torie was sealing the fate of their relationship before it really had a chance to grow. He told himself that her refusal of his proposal signified that they were not destined to be together, not now and not ever. He wanted to cling to the notion that she would change her mind and that, in time, she'd grow to trust in their love, but he felt that his heart could not take the risk. He'd already gone too far with her and he felt that he did not have the strength to go any further without a guarantee. Besides, his boys could not take any more loss.

They hung up without any promises or demands. Monte fought the urge to dial her right back and beg her to reconsider, because doing so would take all that he had left in him.

Once the line went dead, Torie collapsed onto her bed. She sobbed uncontrollably until the well was dry. The only thought that pulled her from her position was the knowledge that she was headed home where her mother's shoulder would be waiting for her to lean on.

Chapter 24

A Friend Indeed

"Hey T., why don't we grab a bite, or a drink, or whatever you're in the mood for?" Martin said as they left the studio.

"I'm sorry, Martin, not tonight. I just want to go home, take a hot bath and get in the middle of my bed," Torie said as she dug inside of her purse in search of her car keys.

Once she pulled them out, Martin snatched them from her hands.

"Hey, what are you doing?" she exclaimed.

"Look, Torie, enough is enough. You've been running that same line for the past two weeks. You've been moping around, keeping to yourself. This is not healthy. Now, I am not going to take no for an answer. Let's just go down to the Grille and have a cup of coffee and talk. You've got to let somebody in, Torie. Please?"

Torie sighed, shaking her head in disbelief. She looked at Martin, whose eyes pleaded with her while he turned the corners of his mouth downward in a frown.

"You are too much, you know that, don't you? Fine, Martin, one cup of coffee and then you will get off my back, or else. Now, give me back my keys. I'm driving."

They ended up at McCullen's, a tiny bar a few blocks from their apartment complex. Martin ordered two Stoli vodka with cranberry juice.

"Torie, I just have to tell you that you are the most amazing woman I know."

"Oh, yeah? Well, I don't feel very amazing these days. I'll tell you that much."

"You should. You are beautiful, talented and an inspiration—"

"Martin, please."

"No, now I'm serious. I'm not just saying these things. I'm saying them because, well, I hate to see what he's doing to you."

"What do you know about it, Martin?" Torie asked wearily.

The bartender placed their drinks in front of them and Torie immediately scooped hers up, taking a grateful sip.

"I only know what I see. He's there and you're here. You're miserable and it doesn't have to be that way."

"Okay, Miss Cleo, why don't you tell me what you see in your little crystal ball or telescope to the stars or whatever it is you use to help people design their futures," Torie said wryly.

"Are you going to be a jerk all night or are you going to listen to me?" Martin asked.

Torie studied his serious countenance for a moment, before nodding her head in concession.

"T., I'm not telling you anything that you don't already know deep down inside. If being with Monte is causing you this much stress, is it really worth it?"

"Martin, it's not as simple as all that. I love Monte, I really do. He's everything a woman could want in a man and I'd be a damn fool to let him go," Torie said emphatically.

"Okay, but answer this—once you get past all the right

reasons why you should be with him, do you ever stop to add up the numerous wrong reasons?"

"Such as?"

"Such as you have a career that is going to take you around the world and back again. You are just about to blow up and you need someone who not only understands that, but can roll with it. Monte's got a family to care for. He's not about to go on the road with you. And after a while, it'll come down to you having to make a choice. I mean, I'm not saying that you can't have your career and love, too. All I'm saying is that you need to be with someone who is of like mind and yoke."

"So you're saying that I should be with someone who's in the business, too?"

"Exactly. Someone who understands what it means to submerse yourself in preparation for playing a particular character. Someone who won't balk at attending industry events, traveling and doing guest spots on late-night television. Monte just doesn't seem like the type."

"Martin, you don't even know him," Torie replied.

Martin closed his fingers around Torie's hand. He gave it a tight squeeze and continued to hold on to it.

"I don't have to know him. I know you. At least, I think that over the past few months of working together, I've gotten to know you pretty well. Tell me that you're happy, T., and I'll back off," Martin said.

Torie wanted to lie. She wanted to pretend that her heart was not breaking right at the moment she sat there talking to Martin, but it was. She hadn't expected to fall in love and certainly hadn't wanted to. Yet, Monte Lewis was the kind of man she'd dreamed of as a young girl fantasizing about her own personal Prince Charming. Unfortunately, she hadn't considered that the notion of happily ever after was not a guarantee.

"I'm not happy, Martin," Torie confessed. "I feel…

I'm confused. I've finally found a man who loves me unconditionally, and I feel like running away. But you're wrong about something, Martin. It's not Monte who's making this difficult. It's me. I can't explain why, but I guess I'm just not ready. He asked me to marry him."

Martin stared at her for a moment, before looking down into his drink.

"Wow, just like that, huh?"

"Yep. He said that he feels like if we make a solid commitment, we can work everything else out."

"And I take it you turned him down?"

There was a hint of hopefulness in his tone that Martin didn't bother to try to disguise.

"Yep. I hurt his feelings, and I feel like crap, but yeah, I told him that I couldn't accept his proposal."

"At least you were honest with him."

"Was I really, Martin? I mean, on the one hand, I'm telling him how much I love him, but on the other... This is all just so messed up."

Torie polished off the rest of her drink and Martin signaled for the bartender to give them another round.

"So where do things stand now?"

"I don't even know. He doesn't call, and when I call him, we talk about the boys, about work, but that's about it. He's distancing himself, I can feel it."

"And?"

"And...and I don't really know how I feel about that. Maybe I already knew from the outset that because our lives are so different, this thing was destined to be short-lived, anyway."

"What's that old saying about how some people come into your life for a reason—"

"And some for a season. Is Monte and my season really over already?"

"I think you know the answer to that," Martin replied softly.

They sat in silence for a while, sipping their cocktails and staring into space. Torie felt like crying, but she'd already learned over the past two weeks that crying would not help matters. All it would do would be to leave her with bloodshot eyes and a headache. By the time she reached the bottom of the glass for the second time, Torie had decided that she was not going to shed another tear. It was time for her to let go and, as painful as that idea was, she realized that she was doing the best thing for both her and Monte.

Though she only felt a warm buzz from the two drinks she'd had, Torie and Martin left her car in front of McCullen's and walked the three blocks back to their building. She didn't want to take any chances and reasoned that she could easily pick the car up the following morning on the way back home from her jog. The night air was cool as they strolled, arm in arm. The silence between them felt comfortable and, for the first time, Torie realized what a good friend Martin had become to her. She'd been missing Lisette terribly, and even though her girl was just a phone call away, it was nice to have someone to sit next to and hold her hand while she vented.

"Martin, thank you for tonight. You really helped me a lot," she told him.

"I don't know how true that is, but you're welcome. I care about you, T., and it hurts me to see you unhappy," Martin answered.

"That's sweet. You're a good guy, you know that?"

Martin let his fingers touch Torie's tentatively at first and then he closed his hand around hers. They strolled the remainder of the way in silence. They said good-night at the door to Torie's apartment and, unbeknownst to her, Martin lingered for several minutes after Torie had shut and locked the door behind her. For Martin, the night had been a success.

His heart continued to beat rapidly from the excitement of being so close to Torie, touching her and providing her with a shoulder to cry on. He could tell that Torie had finally started to see him as more than just a colleague and friend. He'd been elevated to the status of confidant and it was just a matter of time before Torie began to see him in the light in which he saw her. He was convinced that, before long, Monte Lewis would be a distant memory, an unwanted stain on the fabric of Torie's life. She would see that it was Martin who was better suited to give her what she needed. All he had to do was remain patient and loyal. Time would take care of the rest.

Chapter 25

Moving On

Monte lay staring up at the ceiling, silently wishing it would just fall in on him. He immediately chided himself for that thought because, no matter how desperate and grim his life seemed, he knew that his boys and his mother needed him. He could not give in to depression or gloom. As he reminded himself of this fact, however, a part of him resented having to shoulder so much responsibility for other lives on his own. He loved his boys and he loved his mother unconditionally, no doubt. Yet, being strong for them had left no room for him to be weak. He likened the feeling to the athlete playing through his injuries because his team needed a win. Even more appropriate is the civil-rights leader marching his people on to victory even through times when all he wanted to do was just be a regular guy and go golfing with his buddies.

No such concrete words had been shared between him and Torie, but it was understood that the relationship was over. Torie was not willing to make a commitment and Monte was not willing to continue without one. He had never been one for casual dating and, now that he'd been married and widowed, nothing could be truer for him. He'd met a woman, begun spending time with her and he'd fallen hard for her. Monte felt that either they were headed toward something or they weren't.

As the days turned over into weeks without contact, Monte tried to cover up his wounds and prayed that time would heal his broken heart. Unlike when Shawna died, however, there was no sense of finality, no closure. At least back then he was able to stop himself from expecting her phone call or waiting to feel her tossing in the bed beside him. He'd been able to harden himself against hope and dreams because he had the tangible evidence of her departure from his life in the form of an obituary and a death certificate.

The knowledge that Torie was still out there, that her smile was still lighting up the world for everyone but him to see, was a source of great agony. It did nothing to help him forget her. But Monte was skilled at tucking away his feelings and getting on with the business of living. He was a pro, in fact. All he needed to do was to focus on his sons, the care of his mother and his work. If he busied himself enough, he would not have time to think about her, or so he reasoned. Nor would he have time to acknowledge his pain.

"I still can't believe you screwed that up," Brent said.

Monte tossed him a warning look, to which Brent held his palms faceup in surrender.

"Okay, okay. I know you said the subject is off-limits, and I respect that. I just can't believe—"

"That I screwed it up. I know. You can't believe it, Brent, but frankly, I don't really care. It's in the past. I've moved on, so why can't you?" Monte snapped.

Brent held his tongue and focused his attention on the carburetor laid out on the garage floor in front of them. Monte had come over to help him work on the 1967 Chevy Impala car he'd been restoring for the past year.

"Look, man. I didn't mean to bite your head off. It's just that it's been hard enough…you know. I've got to keep my mind pointed forward, not backward. Feel me?"

"Yeah, man. I feel you."

The men worked on, falling into comfortable chatter about the kids and work. They both looked up at the sound of a car pulling up the driveway. It was Pam, Brent's wife, and her friend Chelsey.

"Oh, no. Monte, please don't tell me my husband has roped you into playing around with that hunk of junk in there, too?" Pam said.

Monte stood, rubbing his oil-stained hands on his jeans.

"Hey, Pam, how are you?" he asked, embracing her. "He didn't rope me in. I just thought that I'd better come by here and help him out, or else he'll be working on this car for the rest of his life."

"Well, in that case, how about I fix you some lunch to show my gratitude." Pam laughed. "How are the boys?"

"They're getting bigger and bigger by the minute." Monte chuckled.

"I'll bet they are. Why didn't you bring them with you? You know we love having them. My husband could use some practice at not being the only baby around here."

"I won't touch that one." Monte laughed. "But, anyway, the boys are actually at a birthday party today. I'll bring them next time."

"You'd better. Oh, how rude am I? Monte, I'd like to introduce you to my friend, Chelsey Farmer. Chelsey, this is Monte Lewis."

Monte reached out and took the hand Chelsey offered. He gave it a warm squeeze. Chelsey's warm eyes met Monte's as she offered a smile.

"Chelsey, nice to meet you," Monte said.

"Same here, Monte."

"All right, I'm going to head in and scare up some sandwiches. You two get cleaned up in the next few minutes and come on in."

Pam and Chelsey moved through the garage, entering the house through the door adjacent to the kitchen. Monte watched Chelsey walk away, the sexiness of the woman not lost on him. When the door closed behind them, Monte turned to find Brent studying him, a grin on his face.

"What?"

"Mmm-hmm. I saw that," Brent said.

"Saw what? Man, you're losing it."

"Yeah, okay, tell me I didn't see you checking Chelsey out. It's okay, man, it's just us guys out here," whispered Brent conspiratorially.

"Please." Monte dismissed Brent with a wave of his hand. "Where can I wash my hands?"

"Follow me," Brent said. "By the way, she's single."

Brent smiled innocuously when Monte glared at him.

Over lunch of turkey breast sandwiches and garden salads, Monte allowed himself not to think about Torie. The casual banter at the table created a comfortable mood and Monte found himself laughing for the first time in days.

"So, Chelsey, do I detect an accent—French, maybe?"

"Ah, very perceptive. Actually, it's Creole. I was born in Brussels. My parents and I moved to America when I was seven. I hated it. Promised them that as soon as I turned eighteen, I would be on the first thing smoking back home."

"And what happened?" Monte asked.

"I guess the same thing that happens to most young immigrant girls—I fell in love with pop singers, sports figures and Big Mac burgers. I became an American girl. Thought I'd given up my accent, too."

"It's there, just a hint. It's nice," Monte said.

Brent and Pam had moved into the kitchen, clearing the

dishes and remaining food from the table. Monte and Chelsey sat across from each other in the sunroom and fell into easy conversation.

"So, Monte, besides negotiating the terms of contracts for your showbiz clients, what else do you do for fun?"

"Well, there's work and then there's my two boys—they're a handful. Other than kicking it with Brent and helping him out with that clunker out there, that's about it. Why do you ask, Chelsey? Do I look like I need more fun in my life?"

"I wouldn't say that. Although I think a person can never have too much fun."

Monte had not been out of the game so long that he didn't recognize flirting when he saw it. Both he and Chelsey were having a good time with each other, sharing long, lingering looks as well as appreciative sneak glances. He asked himself, why not? Why not get back out there? The alternative was a depressing one that he'd rather not consider.

As evening wore on and Monte prepared to pick the boys up from their party, he decided to bite the bullet. When he asked Chelsey if she'd like to have dinner with him sometime, it was as if she'd been anticipating his question. Her response was quick and delivered with a smile, and after an exchange of telephone numbers, Monte said good-night. He drove home reaffirming to himself that he was doing the right thing. It was time for him to move on.

Chapter 26

At a Standstill

Days merged into weeks, passing quickly as Torie submersed herself in the show and in reading scripts for other acting parts. She told herself that work was the cure for what ailed her and she was determined to be cured. Unfortunately, the mind cannot always convince the heart to feel the same way, and her thoughts and desires had remained in New York City with Monte.

But Torie had suffered at the hands of love before, and this time she felt stronger and more capable of moving on. When Kevin, who she'd believed to be her soul mate, had stomped on her love, she was young in more ways than one. She'd had an idealized view of commitment and faithfulness. This time she was able to view the situation from a standpoint of maturity. She understood how two people who seemed so right for each other, who'd opened up and discovered incredible passion and connection, would have to put those feelings aside if the circumstances warranted. Geographics, logistics, goals and life plans did not always mesh seamlessly with love. Torie accepted that intellectual reasoning as an almost perfect anecdote for her distress. Almost.

Then there was Martin. Despite her fierce independence, Torie found herself leaning on Martin more and more. For his part, he was a willing confidant and friend. There were days when Torie thought she wanted to be alone, but the moment she closed the door from inside her apartment, she would be filled with nervous energy. Neither hot showers, bubble baths in the hot tub or a pint of rum-raisin Häagen-Dazs ice cream would do it for her. She'd find herself picking up the phone to call Martin, or else he'd already be knocking on her door.

One evening, as they sat on Torie's couch watching *X-Men* for the fifth time, Martin felt as if the moment was finally right to show Torie just how much of a friend he wanted to be to her. He studied her profile, loving the way her jaw moved as she crunched on buttered popcorn. He hesitated momentarily, before reaching over and began rubbing the back of her neck.

"Your muscles are so tense. You need a massage," he said.

"Yeah, I was actually thinking about going to that spa Lana's always talking about."

"You don't have to do all that," Martin said, wiggling his fingers. "I've got you."

He placed his hands on either side of the base of Torie's neck and pressed down firmly.

"Ouch," she exclaimed. "You're supposed to work the tension out, not break my neck."

"Sorry, T., but no pain, no gain. Now sit still," Martin commanded.

Torie closed her eyes as Martin worked the muscles in her neck and shoulders. She could literally feel her body loosening up beneath his touch. She'd always been a firm believer in the philosophy that the human body needed human touch in order to stay at peek performance. No amount of elliptical machines and treadmills could do what the touch of a pair of hands could. Her mind quickly flashed on Monte's hands and the way he used to work magic on her body. She immediately pushed that thought out of her mind.

"Feels good, huh?" Martin whispered in her ear.

"Mmm-hmm. You should go into business," Torie answered dreamily.

She felt Martin's breath coming in short bursts against her ear as his fingers moved around her shoulders and down her arms. She squeezed her eyes more tightly, allowing the soothing sensations to flow through her body. Martin's lips brushed her neck and an image of Monte's lips on her body caused her to tremble. Torie pulled away from Martin, shame flushing her cheeks. She jumped up from the sofa, smoothing the front of her disheveled T-shirt.

"Oh, my God, Martin—," she stammered.

"It's okay, it's okay," Martin said, rising to his feet.

He took Torie's hands in his and attempted to pull her back into his arms.

"No, it's not okay. This…this is not okay."

"T., really, just come here. Let's just sit back down," Martin said.

"No, Martin…I'm sorry, but I think you'd better leave."

"Come on, Torie, don't do this. We were having such a good time. We can just watch another movie."

"No, Martin, it's late…I'm tired. I need to go to bed—alone," she added when a hopeful glint showed itself in Martin's eyes.

Martin moved toward the door. He stopped, keeping his back toward Torie.

"T., you know how much I care about you. I'd do anything for you…have your back whenever you need me. But I can't pretend that I don't want more than friendship."

"And I can't pretend that I'm not still in love with Monte. I'm sorry, Martin."

Without another word, Martin opened the door and left, closing it softly behind him. Torie stood staring after him for a long time. Finally, she turned the television off, locked the door and went to bed. As she pulled the covers up over her body, she wiped away the tears that had begun to flow down her cheeks and hugged herself tightly.

"God, I should be happy right now. This is my dream, this is what I've worked for. Why can't I just be happy?" Torie whispered in the dark of her room. She fell asleep as she waited for an answer that would not come.

Chapter 27

Ghosts of the Past

"Nah, Torie, I can't agree with you on this one," Darius said.

Torie held the phone away from her face for a moment, releasing a sigh of frustration that was not intended for her brother, but that needed to come out of her all of the same.

"Darius, I know that you don't like to talk about him, and I know that you never even really knew him, but he wasn't always the way he is now. The way you knew him."

"I don't care, Torie. Look, sis, this is your thing...your struggle. Whatever you're going through, or think you need to find, you're going to have to do it without me," Darius said, a bit more harshly than he'd intended. "I'm sorry," he added.

Torie considered her brother's words, empathizing with them even through her disappointment.

"I understand," she said at last.

"It's just that I'm about to become a father, Torie, and when I lay my head against Sheila's belly, listening to my baby move around, I know that not even the devil himself could keep me away from that baby. I will never understand why he left us,

Torie. No matter what his excuses are, they will never be able to make me understand that."

Darius's heartfelt statement was more than he'd ever expressed to Torie before. It hurt to hear how pained her brother still was over their father's abandonment. Torie realized that as the eldest there was more that she should have done to help Darius address his anger and his pain as they were growing up. Yet, intellectually she knew that she was too hurt and wounded herself to have been much of a comfort to him.

"Like I said, I do understand, Darius. I might be tricking myself into believing that I need to talk to him or that it will do me any good, but I guess I won't know until I do. I'm out here in California with nothing but a few miles separating me from knowing," Torie said.

Her brother wished her good luck before they hung up. While she was disappointed that he would not accompany her on this trip, she truly did understand and respect his reasons. She called her father and, as if he knew this day was coming, he invited her to his home in Englewood that afternoon. During the drive out there, Torie practiced what she would say, the questions she would ask. She couldn't think of how she would express to him how his absence had shaped her life and was still affecting her.

When she arrived, he was standing on his front porch. Although she had not seen him in years, she recognized him immediately. He was older, seemed a little smaller than she remembered, but that was about it. She parked against the curb and approached the house slowly. It was a small, colorful bungalow-style house, with potted plants lining the short pink-and-purple gravel-filled driveway. It was just after noon and the sun was shining brightly above the houses.

"Torie," he said.

"Daddy," she answered.

They stood in awkward silence for a couple of minutes.

"Come on in," he said.

Hanif Turner led the way into a small, sparsely furnished living room. Torie took a seat on the brown tweed sofa while he settled into a brown leather La-Z-Boy recliner chair after offering her a cool drink, which she refused. Torie glanced around the room, which contained a floor-model wide-screened television, an ottoman in front of the La-Z-Boy and a small bookshelf. When she turned her attention back to her father, he was studying her.

"You look just like your mother," he said when she caught his eye.

"Yeah, I know."

"Man, she was something. I used to watch her up on stage, singing songs like the words were born inside her... She was something to see. We would hit one, sometimes two, clubs in a night and, no matter how dirty the dive or how long the drive, she would be smiling and chatting up a storm. She loved being on the road and loved watching her perform."

"Daddy, I, uh, I didn't really come here to talk about all of that," Torie said.

"I know, I know. I guess I'm just an old man always wanting to reminisce about stuff nobody else cares about anymore."

Again, silence fell between them. Torie felt her resentment rising to the surface as Darius's words came to mind. She swallowed those feelings, not wanting to let herself be clouded by anger.

"Daddy, I don't really know what I expected when I came here. I guess I just need to understand what happened, really. I mean, why you haven't tried to stay in touch with Darius and me. It's, like, when you and Mama split up, we split up. Didn't you ever want to know about our lives? How we were doing?"

Hanif turned away from his daughter. He stared down at

his hands, which lay on his lap. He looked across the room, toward a window through which a beautiful clear day was visible. When his eyes returned to his daughter's face, his own stoic expression crumbled.

"Anita, my wife—my second wife—left me five years ago. I guess she got tired of being alone, too."

Torie's face was a ball of confusion. She looked around the room, understanding finally why it was so sparse and almost uninhabited looking. It was clean but barren, as if not much living actually went on there.

"What do you mean?" Torie asked.

Hanif sighed, trying to find the words to have the conversation with his firstborn child that was long overdue but difficult all the same.

"I'm not a very wise man. Not a very smart one, either—book smart or otherwise. I'm just a man. Never really had dreams or big plans. That's what I loved so much about your mother. She knew how to dream big. But it didn't rub off on me."

Torie sat silently, listening to her father and trying to make sense of what he was attempting to convey to her.

"When Brenda's dreams soured on her, falling apart right before her eyes, I should have been able to pick her up and help her put them back together. But I didn't have a clue how to do that. Didn't know the first thing about saving a dream. Eventually, I couldn't stand to look in her eyes and see darkness where there used to be so much light. I left because I knew that she would be better off without me. I had nothing of value or substance to give her—not the ability to dream, not hope."

Torie's breath caught in her throat and remained there. Hanif chewed his bottom lip, staring past the glass of the window into another time.

"You had that same light, that same dreamy look, in your

eyes that your mother had. I never wanted to watch that light go out."

Torie looked around the room again. This time she noticed that on the bookshelves there were no books. Instead, there were three large photo albums.

"Figured the best I could do was to send money to your mother every month and keep my distance."

Torie began to breathe again, filling her lungs with air, one deep gulp at a time. Her heart raced and her throat felt dry.

"Torie, I'm not a man who knows how to really be with another person. I'm not going to blame my own upbringing or the things that my own parents did or didn't do. I just know who I am and who I'm not," Hanif said.

His gaze fell on his daughter's face.

"When you're onstage, you look just like your mother did when she stood in front of a microphone."

Understanding slowly spread across Torie's face. None of the questions she'd practiced mattered anymore; they no longer seemed to fit into the scenario as it existed. She rose to leave, her mind swimming.

"Hear I'm going to be a grandfather soon. Darius is going to be a good father—better than good," he said to Torie's back.

He opened the door for her and watched her walk out of the house and down the driveway. She turned around a few feet from the curb. Tears now flowed freely down her cheeks.

"Never let anybody steal your dreams," Hanif said.

Torie nodded slowly before getting into her car and driving away. She knew that she would never ask her mother why she'd kept her father updated on their lives over the years and had never let on. She understood all that she needed to understand. She also realized that, while the ability to dream was not a right but a privilege, the opportunity to realize one's dream was a blessing. Sometimes the cost was dear, more than you were prepared to pay. Yet, the real challenge came from trying to differentiate between your real dreams and those that were nothing more than smoke-filled illusions.

Chapter 28

No Surrender

Monte picked up the telephone to call Chelsey more than once, yet he could not bring himself to do it. The mere thought of trying to strike up a conversation, wade through the getting-to-know-you pleasantries, zapped him of emotional energy. How in the world could he honestly begin a relationship with someone when he was only half-there? There was a large part of him that could not be in the present when the past was still so vivid. Although he tried to force himself not to think about that part, he knew that it was a fact that he could not completely ignore. He felt bad about possibly having led Chelsey on, but his heart belonged to another.

The days merged into weeks, passing quickly as Monte tried to focus on everything but Torie. Dividing all of his time and attention between raising Joshua and Josiah, caring for his mother and excelling in his career was taking its toll on Monte. Business had always been both an avenue of pleasure and of great success for Monte, and he continued courting and landing big-name clients for the firm and building a reputation as a tough but efficient lawyer. The day that he was offered a partnership should have been the happiest day of his life.

However, as he sat in the conference room with the firm's founding attorneys, he once again had that feeling as if only part of him were present. He struggled to stay in the moment and to focus on what they were saying to him, but his mind wandered to Torie. He thought about how happy she'd be for him if she knew about the offer and he ached from wanting to share it with her.

Slightly more than halfheartedly, Monte accepted the offer. He was so proud of himself and of all that he'd managed to accomplish, yet there was a hole in his heart where the love of a good woman should be. He celebrated his partnership first with Josiah and Joshua, taking them to Hershey Park, Pennsylvania, for a few days. His dreams awakened him at night, leaving him haunted by images of Torie, and his waking moments were no better as they were flooded with memories of their time together. Try as he might to exorcise himself of her, the scent, taste and touch of her were embedded in him. The day that Monte finally accepted the fact that a life without Torie would be a fate equivalent to dying was the first day that Monte was able to sleep through the night without waking. He realized that there was nothing left for him to do but go to her, for better or for worse.

Chapter 29

The Hard Choices

Determined to either win Torie back into his life or to find closure once and for all, Monte wavered between calling her on the telephone or visiting her face-to-face. By the time he made the decision that what he had to say to her must be done in person, life threw another curveball and forced him to put his plans on hold once again. Marva had taken a turn for the worse, and no amount of hopeful thinking was going to change things.

After consultation with his mother's doctor, Monte realized that keeping his mother at home was selfish and not in her best interests. There had been an increasing weakening of the muscles in her lungs and chest, which made it difficult and painful for her to cough and clear her lungs. The doctors warned that her physical condition would continue to deteriorate and that they needed to be on constant guard for pneumonia and other life-threatening conditions. Cheryl had been good to his family, but it was clear that taking care of Marva was a full-time job and required the skill of a trained professional. Physically, his mother was able to do little for herself and it pained him every time he had to help her use the bathroom or wash up. She needed around-the-clock care, and although he'd never thought the day would come when he'd have to admit that he couldn't give his mother everything she needed, it did.

Smithaven Senior Residence was the best in the area. Marva's doctor had several patients in the facility and it came highly recommended. Monte was able to talk to the family members of a few of the doctor's patients and they all swore that placing their elderly loved ones at Smithaven was the best decision they'd made. Monte visited the facility, met with the senior staff members and left with a good feeling. He decided that it was the only thing he could do, which was the easy part. The tough part was telling Joshua and Josiah that yet another woman they loved and who loved them back was leaving their daily lives. Josiah cried while Joshua tried to play tough, although the sadness he felt was written all over his face. Monte held both boys, trying to be a comfort to them but also deriving comfort from them. His tears and pain mingled with theirs and for a while it was difficult to distinguish the adult from the children. Together they grieved for this latest misfortune in their little family, while silently Monte prayed that God would continue to heal their hearts and protect them from any more sorrow. He could not help but feel that, on his own, he was failing in that regard.

It took two weeks before the paperwork and payments were processed and Marva was settled in Smithaven. The Medicare caseworker strongly suggested that Monte consider placing his mother in Parker Place, a state-run senior's facility that cost half as much as Smithaven did. It was all Monte could do not to rip the man's head off of his shoulders for even suggesting that Monte would choose a home for his mother based on the cost. He assured the caseworker that whether Medicare opted to pay a hundred, fifty or zero percent of the costs, his mother would get the best possible care. Period.

Monte knew that his mother would enjoy being strolled around Smithaven's beautiful grounds. He remembered how much of an outdoors person she'd always been. Growing up, she'd never allowed him to sit around in the house watching television or playing video games like a lot of his friends did. She'd take him to the park or for walks around the neighborhood even in the rain. She used to say that being outside during one of God's showers was the only way to really get all the dirt off.

At Smithaven, Marva had her own private suite with a sitting area, a double bed equipped with guardrails and other safety mechanisms, as well as a senior-protected bathroom. Monte and the boys stayed with Marva all day after she was transferred to the facility by the Smithaven ambulance. She was more alert than she had been in days, although Monte had to explain to her several times why she was moving to Smithaven. She ate heartily from the dinner of baked chicken, steamed carrots and red potatoes the resident served her, commenting on how tasty the food was.

As evening fell, Monte read a couple of articles from the newspaper to her while the boys sat on the sofa playing with their handheld games. Marva fell asleep shortly before they left, and reluctantly the Turner men kissed her sleeping forehead and left her in the care of the Smithaven staff.

That night, after tucking the boys into their beds, Monte sat in the darkness of his living room alone, contemplating the past year of his life. He wished for a sign that could tell him that he'd made the right choices for himself, for his boys and for his mother. It had not been an easy time, but it had not been the worst of times he'd experienced. He'd been so fortunate in his life because, without a father's presence, he could have ended up in a variety of bad situations, including imprisoned or dead. But his mother was such a subtle, yet strong and supportive, force. She'd given him the permission to dream big and the mandate to pursue those dreams with dogged determination. She'd given him more love and encouragement than his hands could hold and all he could hope was that, in her final days, he'd given her the same.

He found himself thinking about Shawna, desperately wanting to ask for her opinion. Shawna had always served as a second conscience for him and her judgment was invaluable and never misguided. He missed that. She would never hesitate to tell him when he was right and, with equal honesty, when he was wrong. Monte opened his heart and let his doubts flow out of him. As he sat in the silence of his home, he felt a sense of renewal spread over him. It was as if Shawna had heard his prayers and placed a comforting hand on his shoulder.

Three days later it was a determined Monte who showed up unannounced on Torie's doorstep. It was after eleven o'clock when he arrived. He rang the doorbell and waited, wiping sweaty palms on the black denim jeans he wore. He shrugged his shoulders up and down, like a boxer attempting to remain loose before a bout. Monte was prepared to beg, to plead, to kick and scream if he had to. What he wasn't prepared for, however, was the possibility that Torie had moved on.

"Hey, Monte. Wow, what are you doing here?" Martin said as he swung Torie's apartment door open.

Monte's eyes grazed over Martin's frame, bare from the waist up. Monte pushed the door open farther and stepped inside. Torie, who had been seated on the sofa, jumped up.

"Monte!" she exclaimed.

"What the hell is going on?" he exclaimed.

"Monte...what are you doing here?" Torie asked.

"Yeah, that's what I'd like to know," Martin added, slamming the door shut.

"Yo, man, just shut up."

Monte glared at Martin, the veins in his forehead throbbing and pulsing noticeably.

"Monte, what…why are you here? Why didn't you call first?" Torie hurled questions at Monte. "Is something wrong with the boys? Is it your mother?"

"No, no, the boys are fine, and Mom, well, she's as good as can be expected. Nothing's wrong," he said.

"So what's going on?" Martin asked.

Monte ignored him.

"What's going on?" Torie echoed.

"I need to talk to you."

"Monte, please, I…I can't do this. Last time—"

"Last time I was a real butt hole and I'm sorry. Just please give me an hour, just one hour where you hear me out. After that, if you want me to leave you alone forever, I will."

"Oh, give me a break," Martin said. "Torie, tell this guy to get lost."

Torie looked from Monte to Martin. The uncharacteristic anger in Monte's eyes told her that the situation was becoming more volatile with each passing second.

"Monte, why don't you have a seat so we can talk about this," Torie said to him.

She turned to face Martin, a weak smile on her face.

"Martin—"

"Come on, Torie, just tell him to leave. You don't have to listen to anything he has to say. You don't owe him a damned thing."

"Chump, you're on real thin ice," Monte growled.

"Monte, just sit down," Torie snapped.

"No, thank you. I don't need to sit. I just need to know one thing, Torie. Are you sleeping with this clown?" Monte demanded.

"Clown? Who are you calling a clown when you're the one who showed up here, unannounced, demanding answers. You've got some nerve, buddy," Martin hissed.

"I already told you to shut up, man. Don't make me have to say it again."

"Monte, stop it. Just please stop it," Torie said, moving between the two men.

"Do you want me to throw this guy out of here?" Martin said, sticking out his naked chest in a show of bravado.

Monte threw a snide chuckle toward Martin. He had no concerns about his ability to knock Martin flat on his butt if it came down to it.

"Martin, please...do me a favor. Just go. Go on upstairs and I'll call you later," Torie said.

"What?"

"Please, Martin. Let me talk to Monte alone. It's fine, Martin, really. I'll call you later."

"Yeah, Martin, it's fine," Monte snapped.

Martin kept his eyes trained on Monte's as he moved toward the door. Torie walked with Martin, keeping a hand on his arm as she opened the door.

"Call me," Martin said, squeezing Torie's shoulder meaningful. Monte's blood boiled with envy while he watched this exchange of intimacy. For a moment, the temptation to just leave—run away and lick his wounds—was strong. However, the memory of the lonely nights he'd spent since Torie had been gone wouldn't let him move. He did not come all this way just to be turned away, and he prepared himself to dig in his heels and to fight for her if need be.

"What's going on, Torie, huh?" Monte demanded as soon as she'd closed the door.

She stormed across the room, stopping in front of Monte.

"Monte, you need to calm yourself down and take a seat. You are the one who needs to do some explaining, not me," Torie said.

"I came here because I love you, and I know damned well that you love me. And do you know what else? I don't even care what that idiot was doing here, and I don't care what you've got going on with him. Whatever it is, it can't mean an ounce of what we mean to each other."

"Monte, this is crazy. How dare you just pop up here and bring all this back up. We've moved on, haven't we?" Torie's voice rose with emotion. "You wanted this. You broke up with me, remember?"

"Tell me you don't still love me, Torie. Say it."

Monte knew that he was shouting, but he couldn't control himself. This was the most critical stance Monte had had to take in his life and timidity had no place. Torie turned her back on him. Her body trembled with a mixture of emotions, one of the more dominant being anger.

"How dare you do this to me," she said at last.

"Look at me, Torie."

"No."

"Look at me."

Torie turned around slowly.

"Just tell me you love me. Please, just say it."

"No, Monte. No. Do you have any idea what I've gone through? How I've felt? I went to see my father, Monte," Torie revealed. "Yeah, I actually called him up and went to see him. See, for some crazy reason, I thought that maybe it was wrong for me to put myself and my ambitions before everything and everyone else."

Torie laughed out loud, a derisive laugh that was as embittered as it was astute.

"If I never see Hanif Turner again, that would be absolutely okay with me. But you know what? I will forever be grateful to that man. He made me realize that not only is it not selfish for me to go after my dreams, but for me to do anything else would mean death to my soul. Monte, if I'm not fulfilled within myself, I can't be fulfilled within a relationship. It just won't work."

"I know that, Torie. I mean, I know before that I said I'd support you in your career and then did everything I could to make you feel like you had to choose between me and it. I swear, Torie, that wasn't my intention and...and I couldn't understand why you couldn't see things my way."

"And now you can?"

"Yes, I can because I love you, baby. Past my heart, past my mind. Past all the self-involved sentiments I've expressed. I won't ever stop loving you, Torie."

"Monte—"

"No. Don't say it. I won't listen to it. Tell me that you're angry with me. Tell me how I behaved like a stupid jerk," Monte yelled.

The telephone rang. They ignored it.

"Tell me that I hurt you," Monte continued over the wailing telephone. "Tell me...tell me that you're going to make me pay for this by making you breakfast in bed for the next twenty years."

Torie glared at Monte.

"Baby, just don't tell me that it's too late. I can't believe that. You can't possibly care about Martin."

"Monte, this has absolutely nothing to do with Martin. Martin is...Martin has been a good friend to me."

"Yeah, I'll bet. He looked real friendly up in here," Monte said wryly.

"Monte, stop. He wasn't wearing a shirt because I'd just finished coloring his hair for him. That's it."

Monte closed his mouth, watching Torie walk away from him. She moved to the sofa in slow motion and sat down as if she had the weight of the world on her shoulders. The telephone rang again, but neither of them even looked toward it. Monte had a strong guess as to who was calling, but he swallowed the flash of anger that rose in him. She had said that this was not about Martin, and he had no intention of making it about him.

Monte stood awkwardly for some time, listening to the silence of the room compete with the rapid beating of his heart against his chest. Since she had not thrown him out yet, he took that as a sign that at least she didn't hate him. He moved cautiously to the sofa, sitting beside her. He was close, but did not touch her. Monte waited and prayed.

"Monte," Torie began in a low voice. "What has changed?" she asked.

Monte was stumped for a moment. He studied her face, trying to formulate an articulate answer to her question. He opened his mouth to speak, but closed it almost immediately. He looked down at his hands, up at the ceiling. He racked his brain for something clever and hard-hitting to say to her. He tried to pull from his skills as an attorney and an orator, but came up blank. When he looked at Torie, all thoughts escaped his mind. He reached out tentatively, putting two fingers on the delicate skin beneath her chin, and raised her face toward his. Their eyes met, and as Monte looked into the beautiful hazel eyes that had magnetized him from the first moment he'd gazed into them, his heart found the words that his mind could not articulate.

"I've changed, Torie. I'm not the same man you met on that elevator so many months ago. I'm not that man who believed that he didn't need anyone in his life…who thought that he could live alone and be all right. I thought that I could control my life, control this relationship. I was wrong, Torie, and I'm not afraid to admit that now. I'm not afraid to say that when I met you, I was still holding on to a past life that had me locked into grief and despair. I had shined and polished myself up on the outside, but on the inside I was broken."

Tears spilled from Monte's eyes and from Torie's at almost

the same moment. Monte used his thumb to swipe at the water on Torie's cheek.

"Over these past few weeks I've been praying for clarity and strength. And, Torie, I can see now. I can see how even though life doesn't work out the way we plan, it works out the way God plans. God has given me permission to let go of the past...let go of the doubts."

"Let go of the fear," Torie said softly.

"Yes, and the hurt feelings and the pain. I don't care how complicated this is, and I don't care how long it takes to uncomplicate it. I love you, Torie. My boys love you. I want to spend the rest of my life loving you, taking care of you and supporting your dreams. Please tell me we can do this, Torie. Please give yourself permission to have it all."

The thought of stepping out on faith and taking a chance frightened Torie more than anything she'd ever felt before. Her natural instinct to protect her heart, after all of the pain and stormy seas she'd experienced, was strong. Yet, one look into the eyes of the man who had touched her soul and Torie's defenses were shattered. At that moment, she didn't care about the distance or her career. Monte was truly the love of her life, all men before him having been mere preparation, and Torie realized that living without him would render everything else meaningless.

Their kiss—the pressing of two pairs of lips together, wet faces touching, tears mingling—was the equivalent of the joining of two dynamic forces of nature. Their love was indeed a power to be reckoned with and, together again, they knew that they would allow nothing to tear them apart.

Chapter 30

New Beginnings

Reunited, and it feels so good. Monte sang the lyrics to the old Peaches and Herb classic over and over in his head. Reunited, rejuvenated and rededicated, Monte and Torie set about the task of really testing the waters of a long-distance relationship this time. Unlike their last attempt, they made no promises or demands, other than to take baby steps in the process of planning their lives together. Monte stayed in California for several days, conducting business via e-mail and telephone while Torie worked onset. For the first day or so, they agreed to just enjoy the moment, acquiescing to the spirit of love that told them that they had the right to feel that love and to share it with each other.

"Have I told you that you look absolutely amazing?" Monte said when Torie emerged dressed for the day from the bathroom the morning following his arrival.

They'd spent the night on the sofa, falling asleep after hours of talking. Despite the awkward physical positions of their bodies, they shared the most peaceful night of sleep that either had had in a long time.

Torie spun around in response to Monte's compliment,

showing off the colorful wrap dress she wore that hugged her in all the right places. Her hair was pulled back from her face in a braid and her skin was aglow.

"You've tanned," he noticed.

"Yeah, like I need more color. This Californian sun is a beast. You should see me slapping on sunblock like it's lotion."

Monte moved closer to her, tentatively pulling her into his arms for a kiss. He felt slightly timid, unsure of how slowly or how quickly he should move. Yet, he couldn't get enough of her lips. He pressed his nose against her hair, sucking in the almond scent. He'd missed her more than even he had fully understood.

"Come on, let's get out of here," Torie said suddenly. "Let me show you around my little town before I go to work. Are you hungry?"

"I could eat a little something." Monte smiled, following her closely, his eyes trained on the sensual sway of her body.

They chatted ceaselessly, Torie asking a million questions about the boys, and Monte peppering her with questions about the show. They stopped a block away from Torie's apartment building in front of her candy-apple-red Camaro sportscar.

"Like her?" she asked.

"Very Californian. I bet you look hot as hell in it," Monte said. "I bet you've got brothers crashing their cars and running red lights with you on the road," he joked.

"You know it!" Torie laughed.

By the third night of their reunion, neither one of them could resist the sexual tension that teased them. They gave in to that tension, making love with insurmountable passion and energy. Their lovemaking came from deep within their souls. They pleased each other through the night, making up for lost time with a fervor that could not be tamed.

The morning sun greeted them, peeking through the sheer

curtains like a voyeur. Torie squeezed her eyes shut as she rode Monte to a climax that rivaled the dozen others she'd had over the course of the night. They'd made love more times than either could count, sleeping just enough in between to rejuvenate their bodies. Even in their slumber they remained conscious of each other's bodies, and each time the flames of desire flared up in one of them, the other was ready, willing and able to extinguish it.

"Good morning," Torie said as she collapsed against Monte's chest.

"Is it morning?" Monte answered.

"Mmm-hmm and a good one at that. Look at that beautiful sun rising out there."

"I can't see a damn thing. I think you've loved me blind, girl."

"Humph," Torie said, giving Monte's chin a firm suckling. "That's okay, it's not your eyes I'm interested in, anyway."

Monte closed his eyes as Torie got up and staggered to the bathroom. She moved like an exhausted runner after a marathon. Monte dozed off and on as the sound of the shower running escaped from the bathroom. It was nature's call that aroused him and sent him stumbling into the bathroom after her.

"Baby?" he called as he entered. "I've gotta go."

"Okay, just don't flush."

While Monte relieved himself, he studied Torie's shapely body through the frosted glass of the shower cabinet.

"Baby?" he called.

"Hmm?" she answered.

"Is there room for me in there?" he asked shyly.

Torie didn't respond, but merely pushed the door open and stepped back. The water hit the back of her neck and shoulders, spilling down the front of her body. Monte stepped inside, shutting the door behind him. Suddenly recharged, his member stood at attention, saluting the vision that stood before him. Without another word, he dropped to his knees, placed both hands on Torie's hips and moved her against the wall. When the tip of his tongue entered her sugar walls, he felt her melt all around him. He stirred her like a cup of coffee and, beneath the steady rain of water, she sang a symphony.

Later, as they lay wrapped around each other, Monte knew that after touching and tasting her again, leaving her would be one of the hardest things he'd ever had to do. He pushed those thoughts violently out of his head, wanting instead to savor the time he had with her. Tomorrow would come and be dealt with. Today, all he wanted was to bury himself inside her love and forget that there was a world outside.

In the wee hours of their final night together, body and soul spent, Monte could not sleep. This time, however, it was the overwhelming peace he felt that kept him awake, instead of fear and heartache. As he watched Torie sleep, wrapped in a blanket of tranquility, he prayed again. In tonight's prayer, he thanked God for sending him a second magnificent woman to be his strength and his rock. Beside her unwavering love, Shawna had given him the greatest gift a woman could give in his two boys. Now, God had seen fit to open a new chapter in his life and had told him it was okay to love again. Monte felt that he was the luckiest man alive, despite all of the rocky road behind him and whatever lay ahead.

Parting was surprisingly easy for Monte and Torie, perhaps because they realized that this time they were on solid ground. The night before Monte left, they sat down in what they'd decided would be a weekly checking-in session in which they would each have an opportunity to put everything out in the open.

"You don't have to tell me any more than you feel comfortable telling me," Monte said.

"I know. I just want you to understand that I really never

felt more than friendship toward Martin. I know you never liked him—" Torie said.

"It wasn't really personal, baby. I just knew that he had a thing for you. It was as clear as day."

"Well, that may be true, but he has also been a really good friend to me. He helped me get settled out here—he held my hand and kept my spirits up when I was hurting."

Monte was silent, checking the jealousy that surfaced.

"I'm sorry that you had to feel that kind of pain," he said finally.

Monte's heart flooded with relief, because even though he'd told himself that whatever went down between Torie and Martin didn't matter to him, his male ego needed to know that she was still tied to him on the most basic, natural level. He pulled Torie into his arms, burying his face in the softness of her hair.

"I love you," he whispered.

By the time Torie drove Monte to the airport, they had agreed to remain open and honest about their fears and concerns as they traveled into the next phase of their lives together. Torie couldn't wait until the season wrapped so she could fly back to New York and spend time with the boys, who she missed tremendously. She didn't realize at that moment, but by the time shooting for the first season of the show was over, Torie was fully prepared to call it quits and relocate to New York permanently. She'd grasped the understanding that her career ambitions did not have to be sacrificed to have her personal dreams realized. Perhaps a simple tweaking would make it all work out.

Torie figured that her mother would be upset and disappointed, but she also knew that she wanted to be with Monte and his boys full-time a whole lot more than she wanted Hollywood fame. She decided that even if it meant that her career would not rise to the level she'd always imagined, wherever she landed would be all right as long as she was in the arms of the man she loved.

For his part, Monte was overjoyed that she was willing to give up her dreams for him. However, he was also disheartened at the thought that she would do that. He knew that while she might never feel a moment of regret for that decision, he would. Monte was not willing to let go of the vision of walking her down the red carpet to the Academy Awards show one day, of watching her shine as a noteworthy, celebrated artist. So he quietly set about the task of securing all of their dreams.

Chapter 31

Permission Granted

One month later, Monte boarded the United Airlines flight with a cacophony of emotions running through him. He'd sat Josiah and Joshua down before leaving, deciding to spell things out for his sons as best as he could. They were young, he knew, but in their short lives they had already gone through more loss than some adults ever have to know. He knew that they needed his honesty. They needed him to give them as much assurance as he could so that, no matter what happened, they could always count on the fact that they were loved. Josiah, the youngest and, Monte was coming to learn, the more sensitive of his two sons, wanted to know if their mother and grandmother still loved them, even though they weren't active in their lives.

"Of course, they do. You can't stop the kind of love mommies and grandmas have," Monte told them.

"I know," Josiah said. "I just wanted to make sure *you* knew."

The wisdom of his children renewed Monte's sense of purpose. He told the boys that he was going to California again to tell Torie face-to-face that, because the three of them love her so much, they want her to be a part of their family forever. Both Josiah's and Joshua's faces lit up at this revelation, much as Monte had suspected. Torie had left as indelible a mark on them as she had on him.

"So, Daddy, are you going to get Torie to move back here and move in with us?" Joshua asked practically, wanting particulars.

"Well, why don't you just hold on and let Daddy work out all of the details. Your pops is putting together a plan that's going to make us all very happy. Trust me."

Once in the air, Monte was surprised by the lack of nervousness he felt. It was as if he knew deep inside that everything was going to work out just the way it was supposed to. He had faith in his love for Torie and in hers for his. All he needed to do was to show her how willing he was to move mountains to make all of their dreams come true. She'd stepped out on faith and let him back in and now it was time for him to make good on the promises he'd made to her. There was no way he was going to let her give up her career aspirations for them to be together.

Monte was busy from the moment the wheels of his plane touched ground. He'd arranged to have a car service pick him up from Bob Hope Airport and take him directly out to Bel Air. Paul Socci, of Socci Real Estate Services, a real-estate agent whose name he'd gotten from a client who lived in California, met him at the site. The property was three acres of land set at the end of a gated, winding private road. He walked around a bit, examining the various trees and hedges that lined the property. He walked in different directions, visualizing the space from as many vantage points as he could. From every direction, it was a beautiful site to behold.

Monte inhaled deeply, a soothing warmth and serenity in the air that answered the unspoken question in his mind. Could he make this place a home for his family? The answer that shouted back to him in the open air was a resounding yes. Joshua and Josiah would love being able to run around in the expanse. He'd have an in-ground swimming pool put in and, who knew, maybe one or both of his boys would become Olympic swimmers. He'd build a small jungle gym and install a swing set so that, when he and Torie decided to have a child together, there would be a place for that child to exercise and run wild. There was more than enough room for all that Monte had in mind, and as he placed his signature on the contracts the agent laid on the hood of his car, he calculated his next move with assurance.

"Hello?" Torie answered breathlessly.

It was just after eight o'clock in the morning and she'd returned to her apartment from her run to the sound of a ringing telephone. For the past few days, she'd been packing up the apartment and making plans to go back to New York. It was with great difficulty that she'd tucked the contract extension she'd received from the network into one of her suitcases without signing it. She'd decided that once she returned to New York, she'd let Monica take care of informing the show of her departure formally, but would speak to the directors, producers and her costars before she left California the following week. It was a bittersweet feeling, but she refused to let herself dwell on that fact. Part of her resolve and optimism had come from an unlikely source and she was still reeling from that fact.

When Torie had called her mother to inform her of the decision she'd made, she was fully prepared to meet resistance and downright disagreement from Brenda. But Torie was also fully prepared to dig in her heels and express to her mother, in no uncertain terms, that not only was she a grown woman, capable of making this decision and all others without her mother's input, she was also very positive that what she was doing in this instance was the right thing.

"You know something, Torie," Brenda began as Torie finished laying out her carefully prepared speech. "I owe you an apology."

Torie was dumbfounded and was unable to find her voice.

"I want you to know that I never doubted your ability to think for yourself and make good decisions for your life, sweetheart. If anything, I think I was afraid to let you go and fly because I couldn't imagine what I'd do with myself. But, baby, I want you to know right now that you are absolutely right. You could not ask for a better, kinder, stronger man than Monte, and if leaving the show and going back to New York is what you need to do, then you go and do it. Everything else will fall into place," Brenda said.

Happy tears streamed down Torie's face as she thanked her mother for her love and support, not only now but all that she had given her throughout her life. Little did Torie know that Monte and Brenda had shared a long talk a few days prior in which Brenda learned just how much Monte loved her daughter. She needed no further convincing to believe that Torie had struck gold in Monte. Needless to say, Lisette had her back and was already out scouting locations for the wedding she was certain would follow soon.

"Sounds like my girl has finally put the puzzle of life together," Lisette had said admiringly, a statement that, to Torie, fit the circumstance perfectly.

Torie slid one of the boxes in her path aside and tucked the handset of the ringing phone between her cheek and her shoulder. She wiped her face and neck with the hand towel she carried.

"Hi, baby," she said at the sound of Monte's voice.

"Hey, yourself. What are you doing?"

"I just came in from my run and I'm a sweaty mess." She laughed.

"I'm sure you're still hot as ever."

"Yeah, right."

"So what have you got planned for the day?" Monte asked.

"Well, right now I'm looking around this apartment trying to figure out how I accumulated so much stuff in so little time and what I'm going to do with it all," Torie said with a sigh. "I'm going to have to ship most of this stuff back to the city because there is no way the airline is going to let me travel with all of this." She laughed.

"Well, why don't you hold off on all of that for a little while," Monte said lightly.

"What? Hold off?"

"Listen, babe. I need you to do me a favor without asking one single question, okay?"

"What are you talking about Monte?" Torie asked, placing one hand on her hip.

"That was a question. Now, are you going to humor me or not?"

"Oh, all right. What do you want me to do? Oops." Torie laughed.

"I want you to listen to my instructions, say yes and then hang up the phone."

"Okay," Torie said slowly.

"I want you to get dressed—casual clothes are fine—and then go downstairs. Outside you'll find a limousine with a terrific guy named Reynoldo driving. I want you to get into the limousine, sit back and relax. All right?"

Torie hesitated, dozens of questions running through her mind. She wanted to ask them all, demand that Monte tell her what he had up his sleeve and refuse to follow his commands until he told her. But because she trusted him with every fiber of her being, she knew that whatever was going on would give her the same pleasure his loving did.

"Yes," she said, before hanging up the telephone.

She bounced into her bedroom like a child on Christmas morning. She quickly laid out a pair of jeans, a plain black T-shirt and a pair of boots. A fan of the long, hot shower, Torie broke from routine and took the fastest rinse-off she'd ever taken in her entire life. Within twenty minutes she was showered, dressed and had fluffed her hair and applied her face. As Monte had reported, there was a Lincoln Navigator limousine outside waiting for her. Reynaldo, the driver, opened the door and helped her settle into the seat. Before closing the door, he handed her a small package. As they pulled away from the curb, soft music filled the comfortable car and Reynaldo suggested she help herself to the glass of champagne he'd poured for her.

Torie excitedly lifted the small package wrapped in golden paper and adorned with a large silver-and-gold bow to her ear. She shook it, sniffed it and, when neither of those efforts revealed anything, she tore into it. Inside was a black stain blindfold and a short note that read, *Put me on.* Torie took a long sip from the champagne flute in the holder in front of her and then tied the blindfold around her head, covering her eyes. She leaned back and listened to the soulful sounds of Sade that issued from the speakers around her. When the limousine finally came to a stop and the door opened, Torie felt a strong hand squeezing hers and pulling her to her feet.

"Monte?" she called.

"Ssh," he whispered in her ear. He held her hand firmly while leading her from the car across a gravel road. Torie stumbled a couple of times as they walked, but Monte caught her each time. He finally removed the blindfold and waved his arms around the empty expanse of land.

"It's ours," he said simply.

Torie blinked, her eyes adjusting to the beautiful bright sky. She looked around, turned to face Monte briefly, before turning around in a full circle again.

"Ours?"

"Yep. We're going to build our home here," he replied.

Torie couldn't believe her ears or her eyes. To say that she was stupefied was an understatement.

"But how? What do you mean?"

She struggled to get the questions out.

Monte wrapped his arms around her waist and pulled her close to him.

"I know you were prepared to pack up your life here and move back to New York for me and the boys, and I could never thank you enough for believing in our love so strongly. But, baby, there is no way on earth I'm going to let you give up your dream. So, I bought this land for us and have hired a landscape and architectural firm, along with an interior decorator, to help build the home of our dreams."

"But what about your job, the boys...their school? I mean, Monte, this is a big decision."

"Well, you know how persuasive I can be. Cooper & Beardsley has an extremely long roster of California-based clients and it's about time we opened up a satellite office here. Guess who's going to head it up?"

"Oh, my God, Monte. Are you serious?"

"Yep. And the boys are bouncing off the walls with the thought of us all being together. They'll adjust to the move just fine, I know it."

Monte beamed at Torie.

"Your mother?" Torie asked.

"Physically, she's as stable as she'll ever be again. The doctors have said that, provided she remains that way, she could make the trip out. I've found a really nice facility here in the county, less than a twenty-minute drive. It's as good, if not better, than Smithaven. I've had to face the fact that the mother who raised me is probably gone forever, but I can at least make her last days comfortable and filled with love and family," Monte said.

Torie smoothed the side of his face, wanting to absorb his pain with her simple touch.

"You are an amazing man, Monte Lewis."

"And you, Miss Torie Turner, are a phenomenal woman. I love you," he said, leaning down to kiss her sensuously.

"So, what do you say?" Monte asked.

"I say, welcome home, Monte." Torie smiled.

"Welcome home, Torie," he echoed.

Monte kissed her deeply.

"Now, there's just one more minor thing." He smiled.

Torie threw her hands over her mouth, stifling the scream that rose in her throat as Monte lowered himself to one knee. He reached into his pants pocket and pulled out the most beautiful marquise-cut diamond set in platinum. Her fingers trembled as Monte slid the ring onto her finger.

"Yes," Torie screamed. "Yes, yes, yes!"

"I haven't asked you yet." Monte laughed.

Torie covered her mouth again, bouncing up and down on the balls of her feet.

"Torie Turner, will you—"

"Yes!" she screamed again.

"Will you be my best friend for life?" Monte finished.

He rose, staring into Torie's shining eyes.

"Yes, I will," Torie answered.

Beneath the sunny Californian sky and with tears brimming in his sockets, there was no hesitation or doubt in Monte's heart that he'd been given a second chance at love. Monte felt free from all the things that had weighed him down in the past, free to live a life of love and happiness again. Torie shared that sense of freedom, for with the love of a good man to call her own, she knew that she could and would have it all. Out of the fog of loss and pain, Monte Lewis was made whole again, liberated and uninhibited to love.